SEVEN SEAS ENTERTAINMENT PRESENTS

Magical D...

story and art by OKAYADO

TRANSLATION
Ryan Peterson

ADAPTATION
Shanti Whitesides

LETTERING AND RETOUCH
Laura Heo

COVER DESIGN
Nicky Lim

PROOFREADER
Janet Houck

ASSISTANT EDITOR
Jenn Grunigen

PRODUCTION ASSISTANT
CK Russell

PRODUCTION MANAGER
Lissa Pattillo

EDITOR-IN-CHIEF
Adam Arnold

PUBLISHER
Jason DeAngelis

Seven Seas books may be purchased in bulk for promotional, educational, or business use. Please contact your local bookseller or the Macmillan Corporate and Premium Sales Department at 1-800-221-7945, extension 5442, or by e-mail at MacmillanSpecialMarkets@macmillan.com.

ISBN: 978-1-626927-50-6

Printed in Canada

First Printing: January 2018

10 9 8 7 6 5 4 3 2 1

FOLLOW US ONLINE: *www.sevenseasentertainment.com*

READING DIRECTIONS

This book reads from ***right to left***, Japanese style. If this is your first time reading manga, you start reading from the top right panel on each page and take it from there. If you get lost, just follow the numbered diagram here. It may seem backwards at first, but you'll get the hang of it! Have fun!!

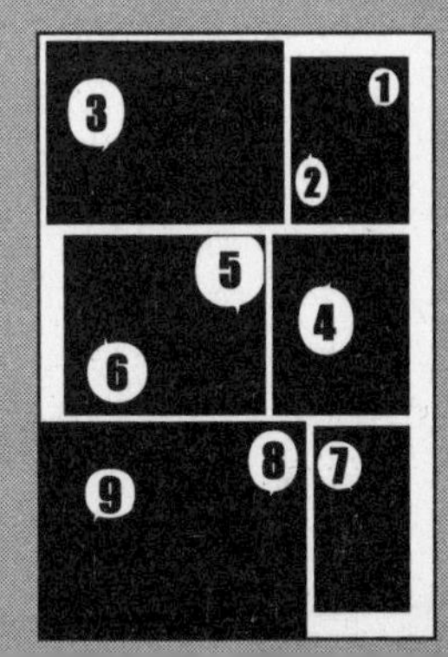

See all **SEVEN SEAS** has to offer at **gomanga.com**

Follow us on Twitter & Facebook!
@gomanga

Chapter 1
Toudou Mako Makes Her Grand Entrance!

THANKS SO MUCH FOR ALWAYS DONATING TO OUR CAUSE!!
NO NEED TO THANK ME. IT'S KINDA LIKE MY HOBBY.

FOUND HIM. THAT'S MY MAN, ALL RIGHT.

PREPARE YOUR-SELF, BOY.
YOUR SOUL BELONGS TO TOUDOU MAKO!!

MAMAMA
Magical Director Mako-chan's Magical Guidance
story & art by OKAYADO
Chapter 1: Toudou Mako Makes Her Grand Entrance!

MA★MA★MA

MAG… TOR

MAKO-CHAN'S MAGICAL GUIDANCE

MAMAMA
TOUDOU MAKO
MAGIC
STAMINA
LUCK
SPIRIT
INTELLIGENCE
STATUS
Magic: 5 Stamina: 3 Spirit: 4 Intelligence: 5 Luck: 1
A prim and proper honor student who holds fiercely to her position as the top student in her class. She can come off as a bit overbearing, as she's hard on everyone (including herself), but she truly cares about and stands up for others and is trusted in turn.
Since she holds the position of class president of class 3-A, most people refer to her as "Class President," or "Class Prez." To her, this role isn't merely a position, but a medal of honor signifying her hard work and triumphs. Because of this, she prefers being called by her position rather than her name.
She is such a brilliant student that her grades are in the top five for each subject. However, this achievement doesn't come from natural-born genius but is rather the fruit of her intensive studying. That said, she's never earned the #1 spot in any subject and she secretly cherishes concerns over not having a subject at which she truly excels or enjoys.
TOUDOU MAKO
★ BIRTHDAY
November 2 (Tights Day)
★ THREE SIZES
75-56-79 (just barely manages to qualify for a B cup)
★ BLOOD TYPE
A
★ LIKES
Studying, Mephisto-sama
★ DISLIKES
Boys
★ HOBBY
Reading
★ SPECIALTY
Speed-reading magic textbooks
★ BEST SUBJECT
Good at all subjects
★ WORST SUBJECT
None
★ MAGIC ELEMENT
Void
ADVANCED MAGIC Textbook of Magic
MP 3000
TOUDOU MAKO

The Magic Realm, Black Lion Magical Academy
VWOM
SCHOOL BROADCAST
BROOM EMPORIUM
ホウキ屋
ATTENTION ALL STUDENTS WHO ARE ELIGIBLE FOR GRADUATION.
THE SUBJECT OF YOUR FINAL EXAM WILL NOW BE ANNOUNCED.
YOUR FINAL EXAM WILL BE...!!

FLASH
SOUL HUNTING IN THE HUMAN REALM!!

YOU HAVE BEEN GRANTED SPECIAL DISPENSATION TO MOVE FREELY BETWEEN THE MAGIC REALM AND THE HUMAN REALM!!
WHOA.
THE HUMAN REALM, HUH?
YOUR FINAL SCORE WILL BE DETERMINED BY THE QUALITY OF THE SOUL YOU CAPTURE!!

CURRENTLY LEADING THE SCORE-BOARDS IS...!!
3-A CLASS PRESIDENT TOUDOU MAKO
3-Aクラス委員長
藤堂魔子
TODOMAKO
500 Point /500
3-A CLASS PRESIDENT TOUDOU MAKO-SAN WITH 500 OUT OF 500 POINTS!!
DA-DAN
I RECOM-MEND ALL STUDENTS FOLLOW TOUDOU-SAN'S EXAMPLE!!
THE HECK ?!
MURMUR
MURMUR
"500 OUT OF 500" ?!
MURMUR
SPROING

CLASS PREZ!
HAYAMI-SAN, TAMAYA-SAN.
WHAT'S UP?
"WHAT'S UP"? YOU'RE TOP IN CLASS IS WHAT'S UP!!
YEAH! 500 OUT OF 500? THAT'S INCREDIBLE!!
OH, IT'S NOTHING.
Man, and so humble, too!
You rock! I'm so jealous!

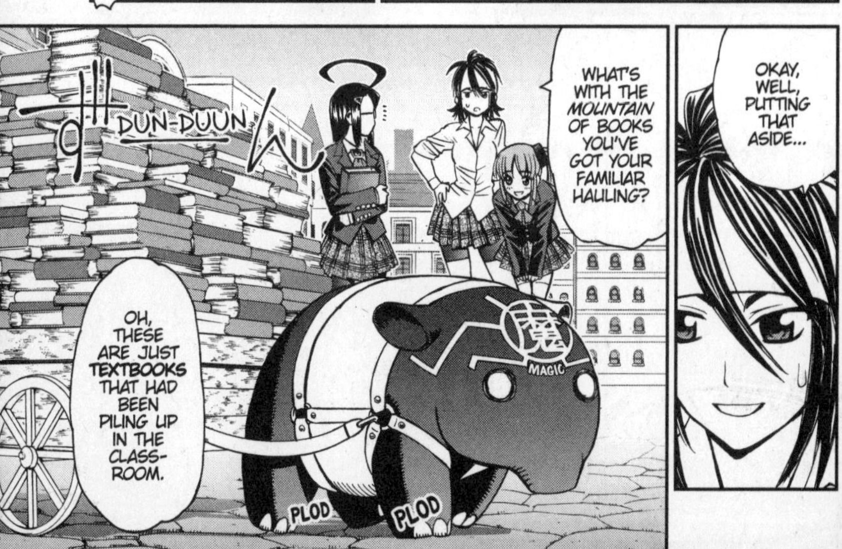
OKAY, WELL, PUTTING THAT ASIDE...
WHAT'S WITH THE MOUNTAIN OF BOOKS YOU'VE GOT YOUR FAMILIAR HAULING?
DUN-DUUN
OH, THESE ARE JUST TEXTBOOKS THAT HAD BEEN PILING UP IN THE CLASSROOM.
MAGIC
PLOD
PLOD

OUR HOMEROOM TEACHER'S JUST BEEN LEAVING THEM LYING AROUND, SO I'M OFF TO THE LIBRARY TO RETURN THEM MYSELF!
HOW CAN A HOMEROOM TEACHER BE SUCH A *SLOB?!*
HE'S A FAILURE AS AN EDUCATOR ...!!
RMB
RMB
RMB
RMB
RMB
RMB
RMB
AAAND SHE'S OFF.

HANG IN THERE, OKAY?
I KNOW THEY'RE HEAVY, BUT YOU CAN DO IT.

MNCH MNCH
MNCH

But she's so sweet.
I know, right?

LIBRARY
YOU TWO DIDN'T HAVE TO COME ALL THE WAY TO THE LIBRARY WITH ME.
NO BIGGIE. I HAD NOTHING BETTER TO DO, ANYWAY.
AND I JUST KINDA TAGGED ALONG.

SHEESH... SHOULDN'T YOU BE THINKING ABOUT THE FINAL EXAM?
You guys need to focus.

I SEEM TO RECALL THAT YOUR GRADES AREN'T THE STRONGEST, HM?
URGH!
I-I CAN'T GET OVER THE WAY YOU JUGGLE YOUR WORK AS CLASS PRESIDENT AND YOUR SCHOOLWORK!
ACK!
AND YET, YOUR GRADES ARE STILL SO GOOD! YOU'RE SOMETHING ELSE!!
GULP!
AT THIS RATE, YOU'VE GOT VALEDICTORIAN IN THE BAG AS LONG AS YOU PASS THE FINAL!

WE'LL SEE.
THAT'S RIGHT... THE TITLE OF VALEDICTORIAN IS NEARLY WITHIN MY GRASP...!!
IF I CAN ACHIEVE THAT, THEN I CAN LEVERAGE THAT POSITION...

TO BECOME THE PUPIL OF THE LEGENDARY MAGE...
MAGIC
MEPHISTO-SAMA!!

IF I COULD STUDY UNDER SUCH A POWERFUL MAGE...!!
HEY, DIDJA HEAR? MEPHISTO-SAMA IS A TOTAL BABE!
AWWW, YEAH! THEY SAY HE'S GOT THE HOTTEST BRAINS AND BOD IN THE MAGIC REALM.

IF I COULD STUDY UNDER HIM ...!!!
YOU MUST BE MAKO-KUN, THE VALE-DICTORIAN. IT'S A PLEASURE TO MEET YOU.
YOU'RE THE MOST AMAZING STUDENT I'VE EVER HAD.
I SHALL BESTOW ALL MY WISDOM UPON YOU.
MAKO. VISION
BA-DUMP
BA-DUMP

SAY, CLASS PREZ.
WH --?!
STARTLE
WHAT IS IT?
YOU GOT A PLAN FOR FINDING A GOOD HUMAN SOUL?
VNN
OH, NO WORRIES THERE. I'VE ALREADY FOUND ONE.
WHA ?!

ONODERA JUN, EIGHTEEN YEARS OLD!
HE'S A RARE, GRADE-A GOODY-TWO-SHOES!!
小野寺 純
ONODERA JUN
KIIIIIN
HOW THE HECK DID YOU FIND ONE OF THOSE ?!
HEE HEE HEE...
DOMINATE THE INFORMATION AND YOU DOMINATE THE EXAM!!
I DIDN'T EXPECT YOU TO BE QUITE THIS ANAL!
BOING
BOING
SO, THAT'S YOUR SECRET TO STAYING ON TOP...!
MY, MY!
CLACK
YOU'RE AS CRAFTY AS EVER, CLASS PREZ!!
DU-DUN

WELL, IF IT ISN'T TAKA-SHIRO MIRA-SAN.
THE PER-PETUAL RUN-NER-UP.
I'D RATHER BE PRE-PARED THAN ALWAYS ONE STEP BEHIND, LIKE YOU.
SHUT UP!! YOU THINK YOU'RE SUCH HOT STUFF!!
WHAT GOOD IS JUST *FINDING* THE SOUL?!
THE REAL TRICK IS **OBTAINING** THE SOUL AND PER-FORMING THE "SOUL PACT"!!
I WONDER, CLASS PREZ, IF YOU CAN REALLY PULL THAT OFF!
WHAT'S THAT SUP-POSED TO MEAN?
WELL, TO PERFORM THE SOUL PACT RITUAL, YOU NEED TO **KISS** THE SUBJECT OF THE PACT!
WON'T THAT BE A ***WEE*** CHALLENGE FOR OUR VIRGINAL CLASS PREZ?

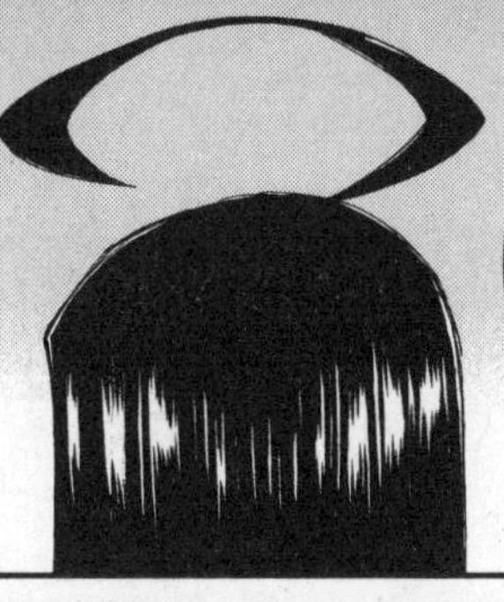
HUH?

WHAT ARE YOU TALKING ABOUT?
WHAT IDIOT IN THIS DAY AND AGE MAKES A FUSS OVER ONE LITTLE KISS?
I mean, I'd be a little hesitant, maybe.
Right?
HUH?!
BUT GIRLS LIKE YOU ALWAYS THROW A FIT OVER THAT STUFF!

JUST WHAT KIND OF CLASS PREZ STOCK CHARACTER DO YOU THINK I AM?
HEY! HOLD IT RIGHT THERE!
CLOP
CLOP

D-DON'T TELL ME YOU'RE TRYING TO RUN AWAY...

MAKO-CHAN ~?!
TWITCH

DID YOU JUST CALL ME "MAKO-CHAN"...?
HOO BOY !!
?
TAKA-SHIRO-SAN, YOU'VE REALLY PUT YOUR FOOT IN IT NOW!!
RMB RMB RMB RMB RMB RMB
YOU WILL REFER TO ME AS "CLASS PRESI-DENT" !!
GWISH !!
FLINCH
MY IDENTITY AS TOUDOU MAKO...
PALES BESIDE MY IDENTITY AS CLASS PRESIDENT OF BLACK LION MAGIC ACADEMY'S CLASS 3-A!
GWOOOOO
NO ONE CAN OPPOSE THIS TRUTH, NO MATTER WHO THEY MAY BE...!!
UH-OH! LET'S AM-SCRAY.

WH-WHAT THE HELL IS THE BIG DEAL?!
PTOO!
I SERIOUSLY COULDN'T CARE LESS...
KLAK
DID YOU JUST LITTER IN MY PRESENCE ...?!
ME, THE CLASS PRESIDENT-- THE EMBODIMENT OF LAW AND ORDER?!
RMB RMB RMB RMB RMB RMB RMB RMB RMB

YOU HAVE VIOLATED SCHOOL REGULATION CLAUSE 58!!
BY THE POWER VESTED IN ME AS CLASS PRESIDENT...
JAB!!

I SHALL HEREBY DISCIPLINE YOU!!
HEH!
BRING IT, SWEETHEART!!

SOLAR PROMINENCE!!
BY WHAT DEFINITION IS *THIS* DISCIPLINARY ACTION?!
THOOM
I'M GONNA STOP HER!
HEY, WAIT!
YOU KNOW WHENEVER YOU RUN, YOU--
DASH
SHFF
SHFF
OOO, CLASS PREZ ISN'T JOKING AROUND...
IT'S ABOUT TO GET REAL!
KYA?!
STUB
WAAH!!

SMACK
VNN
OOF!
!!
FLASH
HUH ...?
THR-KOON
KYAAA!
WAAH ?!

FWOOO
OOOOOOOOOOO
OH, MAN.
THERE SHE GOES AGAIN.
IT'S GOT TO BE ROUGH HAVING A **BODY** LIKE THAT...
...TRIGGERING **MAGICAL EXPLOSIONS** WHENEVER SHE TRIPS AND FALLS.
TWITCH
TWITCH
TWITCH
TWITCH
OWWIE!
NOT AGAIN...
YOU ALL RIGHT, CLASS PREZ?
Not a scratch.
RAN FOR **COVER**, I SEE.
WELL, WHAT-EVER. I'M GOING TO HEAD OUT.
WHA?! ALREADY?!
OF COURSE! I CAN'T STAND AROUND TWIDDLING MY THUMBS IF I WANT TO MAKE VALEDICTO-RIAN!!

POIK
SAY, MIND IF I TAG ALONG AND SHADOW YOU?
OOH. I'D LIKE THAT, TOO!
DENIED!!
RAAAR!
WHA ?!

YOU *KNOW* THIS IS NO TIME TO BE FOOLING AROUND, DON'T YOU?!
YOU GIRLS NEED TO FIND SOULS OF YOUR OWN, AND FAST!!

I DON'T SEE WHY THIS IS SUDDENLY SUCH A BIG DEAL...
YOU'VE NEVER HAD A PROBLEM LETTING US TAG ALONG BEFORE.
SNIFFLE
...!!

AND SO, I CAME TO THE HUMAN REALM ALL BY MYSELF...
IT'S CROWDED, THE AIR IS FOUL, AND THERE'S VERY LITTLE MANA.
HOW CAN ANYONE LIVE HERE...?

I DON'T WANT TO STICK AROUND THIS DUMP TOO LONG!
BETTER GET THIS OVER WITH QUICK SO I CAN HEAD BACK TO THE MAGIC REALM.
SUMMON
VNN

SUMMON FAMILIAR !!
KYUU
SHAA

DEMON SPIDER, AT YOUR COM-MAND !!
MAGIC
WHAT IS YOUR BIDDING, MY MASTER ?!

FAILURE IS ABSOLUTELY UNACCEPTABLE.

BECAUSE, YOU SEE...

HIS GDP (GOOD DEED POINTS), WHICH REPRESENTS THE NUMBER OF GOOD DEEDS HE'S PERFORMED IN HIS LIFE...

...HAS MAXED OUT AT 100 OUT OF 100!!

MAX 100 Point

PII

HE'S ESSENTIALLY ONE STEP AWAY FROM BECOMING A SAINT.

I WANT YOU TO GO TO HIS HOME AND AWAIT FURTHER INSTRUCTIONS.
YOU DON'T WANT ME TO CAPTURE HIM RIGHT NOW?

WE CAN'T DO IT DURING THE DAYTIME, DUMMY. PEOPLE WILL SEE US.
XEON
24

WE'LL MAKE OUR MOVE TONIGHT !!

WHEW ...
KA-CLUNK

SCUTTER
SCUTTER
SCUTTER

HUH ?
THWIP
THWIP
THWIP
THWIP

WHA ?!
GWIP
WHOA ?!
TUG
TUG
TUG
WAH ?!
YOINK
GAH!
SHIK
WH--
GA-KRIIP
WAH VHE --?!

HYUSH
THWIP
KA-CLAK
DRIP...

ZWAAM

GOOD EVENING ...!

FWOOO

...?!

SO YOU'RE MR. GOODY-TWO-SHOES...
"ONODERA JUN," I PRESUME?
?!

I'M TOUDOU MAKO, A MAGIC-USER.
GWOOOOOO
MY APOLOGIES FOR THE INTRUSION, BUT...

I'VE COME FOR YOUR SOUL!!

BLANCH!!

THERE'S NO REASON TO BE ALARMED.
PULL

YES, I'M HERE TO TAKE YOUR SOUL, BUT THAT JUST MEANS PUTTING YOU INTO SUSPENDED ANIMATION.
ONCE I'M DONE WITH YOUR SOUL, I'LL RETURN IT IMMEDIATELY.

NOW THEN... CLOSE YOUR EYES...
SUR-RENDER YOUR SPIRIT UNTO MINE...
WITH THIS KISS, THE SOUL PACT DO WE SIGN...!!

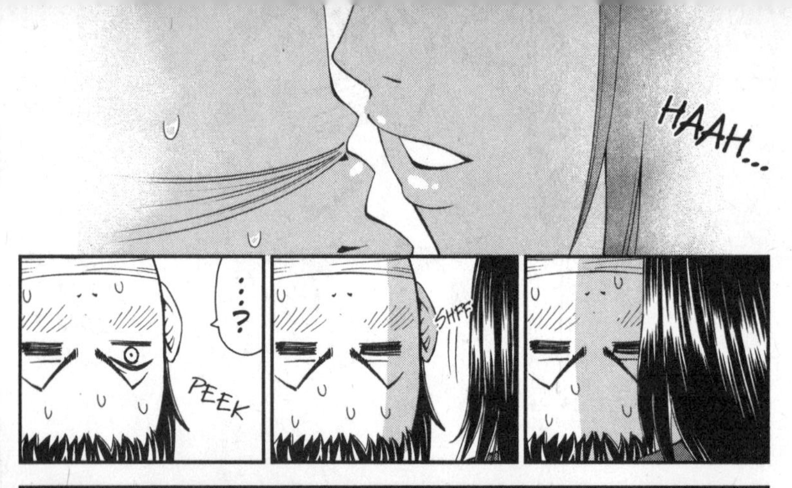
HAAH...
...?
PEEK
SHFF

......
GLOOOOOM
ずーん
?
?

......
I...

I CAN'T DO IT! I CAN'T KISS HIM!!
?
?!
BA-DUMP
BA-DUMP
BA-DUMP
BA-DUMP

"WHAT IDIOT IN THIS DAY AND AGE MAKES A FUSS OVER ONE LITTLE KISS?"
THOSE WERE PRETTY TOUGH WORDS...!
BLUUUUSH
BUT IT TURNS OUT I'M THE IDIOT!!

UUUG
I'M S
PATHE
...!
IF ANYONE WERE TO SEE ME LIKE THIS, I'D JUST DIE...!!

!!
BWOOSH
KYAA ?!
HYUUF

HEY THERE, CLASS PREZ~!
WE DECIDED TO COME SHADOW YOU AFTER ALL!!

WH-WHAT WAS THAT SUDDEN GUST OF WIND ...?!

WH-
WHAT ARE YOU TWO DOING HERE ?!
WEEELL, WE REALLY WANTED TO SEE YOU IN ACTION!
OOO! WERE YOU JUST ABOUT TO MAKE THE PACT?

AWRIGHT! LET'S SEE YOU DO THE PACT RITUAL, THEN!
Eeek! He looked at me!!
THIS ISN'T A SHOW!!
THIS IS EXACTLY WHY I WANTED TO DO THIS ALONE!!

ACK!
SNAG

KYAAAA?!
WOBBLE

WHAT?! AL-READY ?!
YOU'VE GOTTA BE KID-DING...!!

THWACK
SNAP
?!
GA-SLAAM
IT'S ALL RIGHT!
TWITCH
TWITCH
TWITCH
I TRIPPED BUT I DIDN'T HIT THE GROUND, SO WE'RE SAFE!!
ARE YOU TRYING TO KILL MY TICKET TO VALEDIC-TORIAN?!
How is that physically possible?!
LOOK, JUST GET OUT OF HERE!
I'LL HELP YOU WITH YOUR FINAL EXAMS LATER!!
FOR REAL?!

YOU ROCK, CLASS PREZ!!
I LOVE YOU! ♡
GLOOOMP

See you later!

PHEW... THAT WAS A CLOSE ONE.

I NEED TO GET THIS PACT MADE ASAP...
BUT...
GUSH
GUSH
GUSH

I ALMOST FOR-GOT!
RUSTLE

DOMINATE THE INFORMATION AND YOU DOMINATE THE EXAM!! COME TO ME, O WISDOM OF MY PREDECES-SORS!!
BESTOW UNTO THIS HUMBLE NOVICE THE PROPER TECHNIQUE FOR A SIMPLE KISS!!
KISSING FOR DUMMIES
KISSING TECHNIQUE
ROMANTI KISSIN
COMPLETE KISSING
ALL BOUT
BA-BAM

Kissing is an expression of romantic love. A "kiss" refers to the act of one person placing his or her lips in direct contact with the one whom they love in order to show affection...

IT'S NOT LIKE I'M IN LOVE WITH HIM...
KISSING FOR DUMMIES

Let's perform a simple kiss! ♡ First, gaze into the eyes of your darling boyfriend. ♡ Next, express the loving feelings in your heart ♡ and demonstrate them with a kiss. ♡

Let's kiss each other frantically and passionately! Use your teeth to add a special layer of naughtiness!! You can also use your tongue for additional stimulation!

Their lips, crushed against each other in desire, at last began to melt the boundaries between them with sticky fluid... A kiss rife with passion and love. Finally, his frenzied crimson...

HAS EVEN INFORMATION FORSAKEN ME...?
WHAT DO I DO NOW?

UNH...
TWITCH

GUSH
GUSH

......

TUG

IN RETROSPECT... PERHAPS I WAS A LITTLE TOO ROUGH.
THE TITLE OF VALEDICTORIAN MAY BE ON THE LINE...
BUT I SHOULD NEVER HAVE INJURED AN INNOCENT HUMAN.

......
ALL CLEAN!

I'M AFRAID I'LL HAVE TO RETURN TO THE MAGIC REALM FOR NOW...
AND START OVER FROM SCRATCH!

WAIT ...!!

WON'T THAT CAUSE A LOT OF TROUBLE FOR YOU...?
WHEN DID YOU REGAIN CONSCIOUS-NESS?

AND WHAT ARE YOU EVEN SAYING?!
DO YOU HAVE ANY IDEA WHAT SITUATION YOU'RE IN?

NOT A CLUE. BUT...
I DO KNOW AT LEAST THAT YOU'RE IN A BAD SPOT!

I HAVE NO IDEA WHY YOU NEED A KISS SO BADLY...
...BUT I'M HAPPY TO OBLIGE!

H-HOW CAN YOU BE SO GENER-OUS...?
YOU... HAVE NOTHING TO GAIN BY THIS.
"HOW"...? ISN'T IT OBVIOUS?

IT'S A MAN'S DUTY TO HELP A GIRL IN TROUBLE, RIGHT?
BEAM

BA-
DUMP
HAH!
WHAT?! WHY DID MY HEART JUST SKIP A BEAT?!
S-SETTLE DOWN, CLASS PREZ!
A MOMENT OF GALLANTRY IS NO REASON TO GET FLUSTERED ...!!
BLUUUUSH

......!!

ALL... ALL RIGHT.
CLOP
SINCE YOU INSIST...

PLEASE...
ALLOW ME TO MAKE A PACT WITH YOU!!

A-ARE YOU ALL RIGHT?
I-I'M FINE!! WHY?!
NOW, LOOK-- ALL WE'LL BE DOING IS PERFORMING A RITUAL FOR THE SOUL PACT,
SO IT'S NOT LIKE I'M DOING IT OUT OF ANY PERSONAL FEELINGS FOR YOU!
I NEED YOU TO BE COMPLETELY CLEAR ON THAT! EVEN IF I HAD THE SLIGHTEST BLAH BLAH!
GOT IT.
I DON'T WANT YOU TO GET ANY WEIRD IDEAS THAT I RAMBLE RAMBLE!
I GOT IT!
I MUST REMEMBER, THIS IS FOR THE FINAL EXAM...
OKAY, THEN... PLEASE CLOSE YOUR EYES.
EVEN THOUGH I THOUGHT I'D RATHER DIE THAN KISS SOME RANDOM STRANGER...

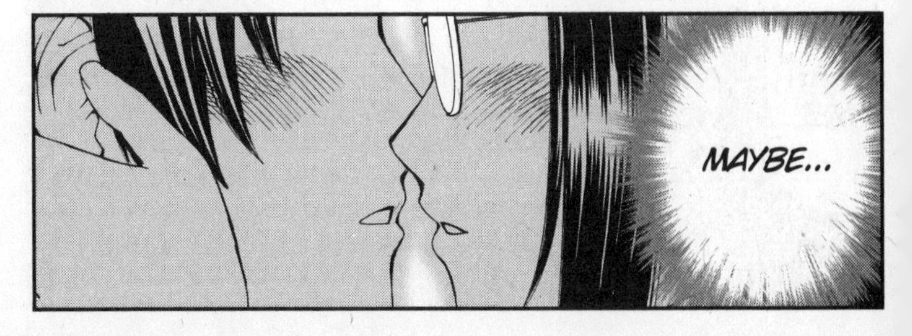
MAYBE...

MAYBE IF HE'S THE ONE I'M KISSING... MAYBE I...
JEEZ, JUNJI! WOULD YOU KEEP IT DOWN?
THE NEIGHBORS ARE GONNA COMPLAIN...
KA-CHAK
CLICK

!!

?!

!!
OH, UHH...

SORRY, JUNJI!
LOOKS LIKE YOUR TWIN BROTHER TOTALLY FAILED TO BUY THE CLUE!!
WHA ?!

WELL, KNOCK YOURSELVES OUT!
B-BROTHER ?!
"JUNJI" ...?!
SLAM

Y-YOU'RE ...

...NOT ONODERA JUN ...?!
VISION
SOUL QUALITY VISION SCAN

WELP, LOOKS LIKE MY COVER'S BLOWN... THAT'S RIGHT!!
I'M JUN'S TWIN BROTHER ...!!
PI
PI
PI
PI
PI
01
Searching---Please wait

"MISTER LIBIDO" HIMSELF!!
WHIRL
WHIRL
ONODERA JUNJI!!
HIS GDP IS ZERO?!
HE'S A GRADE-A RAT BASTARD!!
ONODERA JUNJI
小野寺純次
0 Point
!!

HOW DID I MISS ALL THIS PORN?!
DUUN
DUN
Bad Behavior From Around the World
The Erotic Detective
Shikama Youko's S&M Circus
GIRLS IN THE NUDE

PYOING
OKAY!! GLAD THAT'S CLEARED UP!!
KYAAAAAAA?!
TWUFF
NOW, WHERE WERE WE?!
He can fly?!
HEY!
VNN
EXPLOSION
DON'T FLATTER YOUR-SELF!!
BOOM
GYA!
I CAN'T BELIEVE HOW CARE-LESS I WAS!!
HOW COULD I HAVE MISSED THAT HE HAD A RAT BASTARD FOR A TWIN?!
Ugh...
FIZZLE
FIZZLE
AND HE EVEN TRIED TO PERFORM THE PACT KISS ON HIS OWN INITIATIVE!!!
GASP!
SIZZ
SIZZ

?!!
ULTRASONIC DISROBING TECHNIQUE: SUPER STRIPPER!!
GAAH ?!
COVER
HE'S FAST! ARE HUMANS REALLY CAPABLE OF THIS KIND OF SPEED?!
WHY, YOU ...!
BWAA
MAGIC
HEY NOW! WAIT JUST A SECOND !!
I SUGGEST YOU STRETCH YOUR ARMS OUT...!
SNAP
......?

HOOK HACKER!..
POP

......!!!

NOW YOU'RE TOTALLY HELP-LESS!
WRIGGLE
WRIGGLE
KYAAAA!!!

ALL RIGHT! PUCKER UP!!
WHOOSH

SNAP
?!

WHA ?!
STREEEETCH
SPIDER SILK?!
He He He!

WAAH! AND I WAS SO CLOSE, TOO!!

THIS IS SO PATHETIC... I CAN'T BELIEVE I LET MYSELF GET ALL WORKED UP...
DOES THIS MEAN THAT HIS GALLANTRY FROM BEFORE WAS ALL JUST AN ACT...?
Girls in trouble blah blah blah...

THAT WAS A CLOSE CALL...
This isn't over yet!
JUST IMAGINE WHAT WOULD'VE HAPPENED IF WE'D MADE THE PACT...

HOLD IT RIGHT THERE!!
FLINCH

SORRY, CLASS PREZ!
BUT I WON'T BE LETTING YOU TAKE VALEDICTORIAN THAT EASILY!!
DA-D
THANKS TO LITTLE MISS DETONATOR, WE NEVER DID FINISH OUR CONVERSATION EARLIER!
BUT THIS TIME...

N-NOT BAD, CLASS PREZ!
I DIDN'T EXPECT YOU TO USE YOUR FEMININE WILES ON HIM!!
I-IT'S NOT WHAT YOU THINK ...!
WELL, TWO CAN PLAY AT THAT GAME!!
SAY...
YOU, BOY IN BOND-AGE... ♡
WAIT! HE'S ...!
WANT TO MAKE A PACT WITH ME?
JIGGLE

DWAH !!!
KYAAA !!
LUNGE
He ignored me?!
WHA ?!

HOW COULD YOU BE INDIFFER-ENT TO MY ENOR-MOUS RACK?!
POW

YOU REALLY WANT TO KNOW ...?

IT'S BECAUSE YOUR ENTICE-MENT HAD NO DEPTH TO IT!
GLARE
IT WAS NOTHING BUT CHEAP AND OBVIOUS SEX APPEAL!!
STAB
IF *THAT'S* MY ONLY OTHER OPTION, I CHOOSE THE SHY CLASS PREZ WITH THE ITTY BITTY TITTIES!!!
WHA ?!

SHAKE SHAKE SHAKE SHAKE
S-SO, CLASS PREZ EVEN BEATS ME WHEN IT COMES TO SEX APPEAL ...?!
THAT DOES IT!!
I'LL TAKE YOUR SOUL, EVEN IF I HAVE TO DO IT BY FORCE--!!
THROTTLE
THAT'S ENOUGH !!
STOMP

WE WON'T LET YOU GET IN HER WAY!!
'Cause she's gonna do our exams for us later!!
LITTLE MISS DETON-ATOR AND FRIEND #2!!

I HAVE NO USE FOR EITHER OF YOU!
Begone!!
Never!
HEY, MY GRADE'S AT STAKE HERE, TOO, YA KNOW!
WH-WHAT'RE YOU ALL DOING HERE?
WHOA-AA...!!

GLASSES, BUSTY, SPORTY, AND LOLI!
JACKPOT!
AM I IN HEAVEN ?!
MURR...
HEY!! DON'T LEAVE ME OUT IN THE COLD!!
?!!
SPROING
WHAT THE --?!
SNAP
UGH!
JERK
HUH ...?
BONK
VUNN

FLASH
KA-BOOM

CRUMBLE
CRUMBLE

POIK
CRUMBLE
CRUMBLE

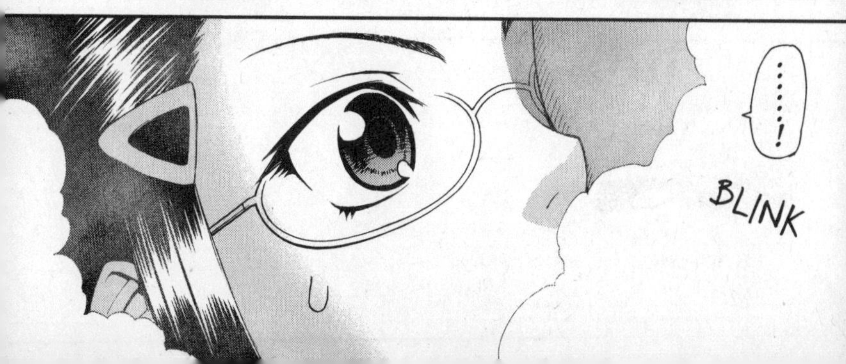

......!
BLINK

......
?!!
SHOVE
THUD
D...

DID WE...
ACCIDEN-TALLY FORM A PACT...?!

NOOOOOOOOOOOO!!!

LIBRARY
LIBRARY
The next morning, in the Magic Academy's Library.

NOT IN HERE ...
TOSS
Call from the abyss

NOT HERE...
OR HERE.
OR HERE!
OR HERE!!
I CAN'T FIND IT ANY-WHERE!!!
TOSS
FLING
TOSS
FLING
TOSS
TOSS
I CAN'T FIND ANY WAY TO BREAK THE SOUL PACT!!
BUT IF I BRING THE EVALUATORS THAT RAT BASTARD'S SOUL...
...THEN GOODBYE VALEDICTORIAN. I MIGHT NOT EVEN GRADUATE...!!
WOBBLE
KERTHUD THUD THUD
KYA?!
IS THAT YOU, CLASS PREZ?
HOW COULD I WASTE MY ONE AND ONLY SOUL PACT CHANCE ON HIM...
SORRY FOR SCREWING UP YOUR PACT LAST NIGHT.
WHEN WE CAME TO, WE WERE BACK HERE IN THE MAGIC REALM, BUT WE STILL HAVE NO CLUE ABOUT...

UUGH
TWITCH
TWITCH
CLASS PREZ !!

IT'S NO USE...I CAN'T FIND IT ANY-WHERE. MEPHISTO-SAMA...
WH-WHAT ON EARTH HAPPENED TO YOU YESTERDAY, CLASS PREZ...?

AND I CAN'T BELIEVE YOU'RE TRAPPED UNDER A PILE OF BOOKS.
I KNOW YOU FOCUS ON HONING YOUR BRAIN, CLASS PREZ, BUT YOU'VE GOTTA WORK OUT YOUR BODY TOO.

......
TWING
WORK OUT?!

HONE ?!

THAT'S IT!
THERE'S STILL A WAY TO FIX THIS!!

CLOP

JUST HOW LONG ARE YOU PLANNING TO BE A LUMP?
KWAM
DUGH!

?!
ALLOW ME TO FORMALLY INTRODUCE MYSELF.
はっ
LURCH

MY NAME IS TOUDOU MAKO!
AND FROM TODAY ONWARD, I WILL BE ON YOU LIKE FLYPAPER TO HONE YOU INTO THE PERFECT GOODY-TWO-SHOES!!
WHA ...?!
YOU'RE GONNA "HONE ME"?!
ON ME LIKE FLY-PAPER ...?!
WAIT! DOES THAT MEAN ...?!

I'LL BE LIVING WITH A GIRL!!
I CAN PEEK IN ON YOU WHILE YOU CHANGE ...
OR RUN INTO YOU WHILE YOU'RE BATHING ?!
BWA HA HA HA HA HA!

AW, YASS! I CAN'T WAIT FOR ALL THE SEXY "ACCIDENTS" WE'LL...
LUNGE
HAVE ?!
SNAG
OABA?!
WHAM
AH!
TUMBLE
OOF!
TUMBLE
NUH!
TUMBLE
BUH!
TUMBLE
STOMP
GWE
!!
I'LL REFORM HIM IF IT'S THE LAST THING I DO!
I WILL BE VALEDIC-TORIAN!!
Actu-ally... this is kinda hot...

STATUS

Magic: 2 Stamina: 5 Spirit: 3 Intelligence: 1 Luck: 4

One of Mako's close friends. Messy, optimistic, and easy-going, but pretty irresponsible. She's something of a problem child who consistently relies on Mako for her schoolwork, but she values friendship more than anything and is secretly a little concerned that Mako is a little too tightly wound.

Even her clothes are sloppy since she only wears an undershirt (with no bra); and while she wears bike shorts under her skirt, this is simply to prevent chafing during broom-riding, and not to protect her from panty shots.

An adrenaline addict who loves speed and thrills on an entirely different level than most, she satisfies her need for speed by flying around on her broomstick whenever she gets a chance. Because of this, she's become so skilled at flying that she's referred to as the "fastest broom-rider on campus." While she holds the top grade in broomstick-riding, she's disastrously poor at all other subjects, and as such is on the verge of being held back. But this fact doesn't really bother her all that much.

HAYAMI SHUN

★ BIRTHDAY

October 10 (formerly P.E. Day)

★ THREE SIZES

86-58-88 (E cup)

★ BLOOD TYPE

O

★ LIKES

Thrills, going fast

★ DISLIKES

Boredom

★ HOBBY

Cruising on her broomstick

★ SPECIALTY

Ultra-fast flight

★ BEST SUBJECT

Broomstick-riding, transformation magic

★ WORST SUBJECT

All other subjects

★ MAGIC ELEMENT

Wind

MP ›››››››› 1500

HAYAMI SHUN

MY NAME IS TOUDOU MAKO.
SHAAAAA
I DON'T MEAN TO SOUND FULL OF MYSELF, BUT...
I'M A TOP STUDENT WITH EXCELLENT GRADES.
I'M THE VERY MODEL OF A CLASS PRESIDENT.
RIGHT NOW, I'M ABOUT TO COMPLETE THE FINAL EXAM AND GRADUATE FROM THE MAGIC ACADEMY.
Ah, so refresh-ed.
PEEK
WHICH IS WHY I'M HERE IN THE HUMAN REALM.
にゃぁあ!!
NYAAA...!
GRAB
MAMA

TO BE PERFECTLY HONEST, I SHOULD'VE RETURNED TO THE MAGIC REALM BY NOW.
VNN
ELECTRICITY
FLINCH
?!
GYABA!!
BRZZT
WHY AM I IN THE HUMAN REALM TO BEGIN WITH, YOU ASK?
KA-CHAK
SIZZLE
SIZZLE
OH, FOR RYING OUT OUD ...
PUTTING UP A MAGIC CIRCLE WAS CLEARLY THE RIGHT DECI-SION ...!
CLACK
I USE YOUR SHOWER FOR ONE MINUTE AND YOU TRY TO SNEAK A PEEK...!

Chapter 2:
A Hard Kiss?!
YOU PERVERT !!
Magical Director Mako-chan's
Magical Guidance

THIS JERK'S NAME IS ONODERA JUNJI.
Itty-bitty titties
SIZZ
SIZZ
I ACCIDENTALLY PERFORMED THE SOUL PACT WITH THIS FIEND AND IT COULD AFFECT MY GRADES...!
Seriously, how did it come to this...?
AS YOU CAN SEE, HE'S A SICK, PERVERTED, RAT BASTARD.
SIZZ
NOW I CAN'T GO BACK TO THE MAGIC REALM UNTIL I TURN HIM INTO A GOOD PERSON!!

GOOD MORNING, TOUDOU-SAN!!
AH, THE RAT BASTARD'S TWIN BROTHER...!

WHOA! WHAT HAPPEN-ED HERE?!
C-COULDN'T SAY...
SIZZ
SIZZ

TA-DAAA!
PLEASE, EAT TO YOUR HEART'S CONTENT !!
EGUMILK

THIS IS ONODERA JUN. THE TWIN BROTHER TO THAT IDIOT AND A CONSUMMATE GOODY-TWO-SHOES.

YOU'RE TOO KIND. I CAME OVER WITHOUT ANY NOTICE AND YET...YOU TREAT ME TO BREAK-FAST.
How many people is this for...?
DON'T EVEN WORRY ABOUT THAT~!

Pardon me, but where are your parents?
They're both overseas on a business trip.

I WAS SUPPOSED TO PERFORM THE SOUL PACT WITH HIM!

IF ONLY I'D MADE THE PACT WITH JUN'S SOUL, I'D HAVE HAD VALEDICTORIAN IN THE BAG...!!

REALLY, IT'S PER-FECTLY FINE!
I'M HAPPY TO MAKE BREAKFAST FOR MY BROTHER'S GIRLFRIEND!
KONK

N-NO, I'M NOT--!!
I'M SO GLAD HE HAS A GIRLFRIEND LIKE YOU~!

YOU SEEM SO HARD-WORKING AND RESPON-SIBLE!
LOOK, I'M TELLING YOU THAT YOU'VE GOT THE WRONG IDEA...

SIGH... HOW CAN TWO BROTHERS BE SO DIFFERENT...?
PANT PANT

BWAM
AND WHAT THE HELL DO YOU THINK *YOU'RE* DOING?!

ERR... I, AH, DROP-PED MY GLASS-ES...
YOU DON'T EVEN *WEAR* GLASSES!!
AHA HA! I'M HAPPY TO SEE YOU TWO ARE SO CLOSE~!
I'M TELLING YOU THAT'S NOT IT--!!

THAT ASIDE, I THOUGHT I HEARD AN EXPLOSION LAST NIGHT...
FLINCH
A-ABOUT THAT...!
AFTER ALL THAT RUCKUS YOU ONLY *THINK* YOU HEARD AN EXPLO-SION?! JUST HOW DENSE *ARE* YOU?!
STOMP

IT WAS INSANE! SHE USED MAGIC TO-- GWOOF?!
WAAAAAH!
TH-CHOP
?
YOU WERE DREAMING!
YOU MUST HAVE BEEN!!
......
L-LET ME BORROW MY SWEETIE FOR JUST A MINUTE!!

HOW MANY TIMES DO I HAVE TO TELL YOU?!
Junji
NO BROTHERS ALLOWED!!
DISCUSSION OF MAGIC IS ABSOLUTELY OFF-LIMITS!!
BRING IT UP AGAIN AND I'LL WHACK YOU UPSIDE THE HEAD WITH MY BROOM!!
DOES THAT SERIOUSLY JUSTIFY KARATE-CHOPPING ME IN THE THROAT ...?!

SUMMON
Summon
REMEMBER HOW I GOT HERE EARLY THIS MORNING TO REPAIR YOUR ROOM SO THAT PEOPLE WOULDN'T CATCH A GLIMPSE OF THE MAGIC?!
MAGIC

Household helper spirits: Brownies
Spirits that can work for you with magic. They're good with their hands, so they can do everything from cooking to home renovation.

IF ANYONE HAD FOUND OUT, I'D HAVE TO LEAVE THE HUMAN REALM!
AND I COULD KISS MY CHANCES OF BEING VALEDICTORIAN GOODBYE!
IT'S ALL RIGHT! JUST LEAVE IT TO ME!!
YOU SEE, I'M UN-STOPPABLE NOW THAT MY LIFE-LONG DREAM HAS BEEN FULFILL-ED!!
DREAM ...?

LIVING WITH A GIRL!!
CLENCH
UGH... HOW LONG AM I GOING TO HAVE TO STAY HERE...?
IF ONLY I'D NEVER MADE THIS STUPID PACT...

PACT?

WHAT'S THIS "PACT"?! YOU MEAN THAT THING WHERE YOU NEEDED TO KISS ME?!
WE KISSED?! YOU AND I?! WHEN?!

DON'T TELL ME YOU DID IT WHILE I WAS UNCON-SCIOUS!
HOW DARE YOU! THAT WAS MY FIRST KISS, YA KNOW!!
WH-WHY ARE YOU YELLING AT ME?!
I'm the one who should be angry!!

IT DOESN'T COUNT IF I WAS OUT COLD!!
BET-TER DO IT AGAIN! ♡
MWAH! ♡
AS IF!!

PLEE-EASE, MAKO-CHAAAN ~!
THROB

RMB RMB RMB RMB RMB RMB RMB
DID YOU JUST CALL ME "MAKO-CHAN" ?!
YOU WILL CALL ME "CLASS PRESI-DENT" !!

BUT IT'S NOT LIKE YOU'RE MY CLASS PRESIDENT.
THAT DOESN'T MATTER !!

I'M HELPING TO GUIDE YOU DOWN THE PROPER PATH IN LIFE!!
POINT
GUIDANCE! THAT'S A CLASS PRESI-DENT'S JOB!!
SMACK
SO I WON'T LET YOU CALL ME BY MY NAME!!
CLENCH
YOU WILL REFER TO ME AS...
CLASS PRESIDENT OF BLACK LION MAGIC ACADEMY'S CLASS 3-A!!
GRAR!

MAGIC ...?

Y-YOU WERE LISTENING?!
I CAN EXPLAIN ...!
OH, DON'T STOP ON MY BEHALF. I'M ABOUT TO HEAD OUT.

OH? WHERE TO?
I VOLUNTEERED TO HELP CLEAN UP THE PARK. WELL, SEE YA!!

SIGH... THAT'S A GENUINE GOODY-TWO-SHOES FOR YOU.
I WISH YOU'D TAKE A PAGE OUT OF HIS...

WE'RE GOING WITH HIM!!
HUH?! WHERE DID THIS COME FROM ALL OF A SUDDEN?!
YOINK

COULD THIS BE...A DATE?!
......

TAMA-
SAKI
PARK

OOO! A DATE IN THE PARK?
But all these volunteers kinda kill the mood.
Plus, my doofus twin's here.
THIS ISN'T A DATE!

WHA?! YOU LIED TO ME?!
SHUT UP AND LISTEN !!

IN ORDER TO BECOME A GOODY-GOODY, IT'S ESSENTIAL THAT YOU INCREASE YOUR GOOD DEEDS SCORE!!
AND VOLUN-TEERING IS A PERFECT EXAMPLE OF A GOOD DEED!!
THERE-FORE, IN ORDER TO MAKE YOU INTO A GOODY-GOODY...
YOU'RE GOING TO BE EARNING GOOD DEED POINTS BY CLEANING THE PARK ALL DAY!!
POINT

YOU CAN YELL ALL YOU LIKE, "CLASS PREZ," BUT I DON'T REMEMBER SAYING I WAS GONNA BECOME A GOOD PERSON.
SULK
WHY, YOU...!!

NOW, IF I GOT SOMETHING IN RETURN, THAT'D BE A DIFFERENT STORY~!
SOME-THING IN RE-TURN?
SMIIIRK
THAT'S RIGHT. FOR EXAMPLE...

HOW ABOUT ...
A NICE FRENCH KISS ?!
LICK

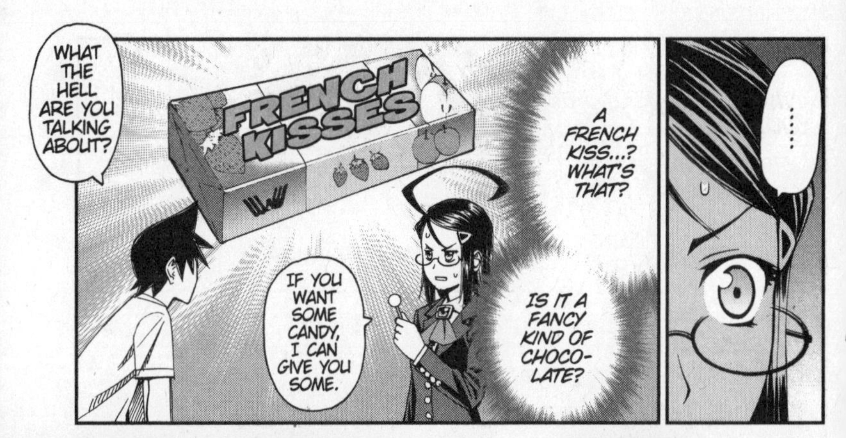
......
A FRENCH KISS...? WHAT'S THAT?
IS IT A FANCY KIND OF CHOCOLATE?
IF YOU WANT SOME CANDY, I CAN GIVE YOU SOME.
WHAT THE HELL ARE YOU TALKING ABOUT?
FRENCH KISSES

WAIT... DON'T TELL ME YOU DON'T *KNOW* WHAT A FRENCH KISS IS?!
O-OF COURSE I DO!!
Oh, really~?
I'M THE TOP HONOR ROLL STUDENT AT MY SCHOOL! THERE'S NOTHING THAT I DON'T KNOW!!
GACK!
F-FINE! IF YOU MAKE THIS PARK SPICK AND SPAN...
I'LL GIVE YOU ONE OF THESE "FRENCH KISSES" !!
SMACK

BOOYAH!
SWEEP SWEEP SWEEP SWEEP SWEEP
IMMA HOLD YOU TO THAT, MAKO-CHAN!!
JOLT
?!
WH-WHAT'S GOT HIM SO PUMPED ...?
FWOOOOO OOOOOOOO
I HOPE I HAVEN'T PROMISED HIM SOMETHING WEIRD.

SUSHI
ON SALE
I THINK IT SHOULD BE SAFE TO USE MAGIC HERE.
GLANCE
GLANCE
ALL RIGHT ...

SEARCH ENGINE MAGIC: MAHOO!!
VWNN
KEY-WORD: "FRENCH KISS."
FRENCH KISS
PI
SEARCH
DISPLAY SEARCH RE...
TKIIII

SULTS?!
FLASH
FLINCH

EEE...
AH...
SUCK
SUCK
SLURP
SLURP
SMACK
SMACK
SLURP
KI...
KYAAAAAA!!
SMACK

OH NO!!
WHAT KIND OF PROMISE HAVE I GONE AND MADE?!!

ONCE HE FINISHES CLEANING, I'LL HAVE TO...!!
WAAA!
SUCK
SLURP
SLURP
SMACK
SUCK
CENSORED
I CAN'T LET THAT HAPPEN!!

BUT WHAT CAN I DO...?
HE'S ACTUALLY DOING A GOOD JOB OF CLEANING. PLUS, HE'S EARNING GOOD DEED POINTS...!
VISION
VNN
IF I STOP HIM, ALL MY HARD WORK WILL HAVE BEEN FOR NOTHING!
GOOD DEED POINTS
善行値
04 Point

BUT I CAN'T HAVE HIM CLEAN WITHOUT GIVING HIM THAT FRENCH KISS I PROMISED...!
ISN'T THERE ANY WAY I CAN HAVE MY CAKE AND EAT IT, TOO?!

HEY! HOW LONG OF A BREAK ARE YOU GONNA TAKE?!
IF YOU SLACK OFF, WE'LL NEVER FINISH CLEANING!
......
NEVER FINISH CLEANING...?
THAT'S IT!!

ALL I HAVE TO DO IS MAKE SURE THE CLEANING NEVER ENDS!
THAT WAY, HIS GOOD DEED POINTS WILL GO UP, AND I WON'T HAVE TO FRENCH KISS HIM!!
KI!!!!
ALL MY FAMILIARS, LEND ME AN EAR!!
YE THREE-SCORE AND TWELVE BOUND FIENDS, I BID THEE APPEAR!!
SUMMON
VUNN

IN ONE MASSIVE ONSLAUGHT, GATHER UP TRASH...!
HIS EFFORTS TO TIDY, I BID THEE TO DASH!!
BWOON!!

Small & Cute
SUMMON

D-DID M SUMMO FAIL?! ALL I WAS ON LITTLE PUPPY ?!
PANT PANT PANT
MAGIC
I'VE NEVER MESSED UP LIKE THIS BEFORE! HOW COULD THIS HAPPEN ...?!

Hellhound (puppy)

A dog whose natural habitat is Hell. Its drool is poisonous and those who are bitten by it go insane.

AH! HOW COULD I HAVE FORGOTTEN?! MANA IS THINNER HERE IN THE HUMAN REALM.
THAT'S WHY MY SUMMON FAILED...!
Plus, I stayed up all night and didn't eat any breakfast...

WELL, NOW WHAT SHOULD I DO...? THERE'S NO WAY A SINGLE PUPPY CAN GATHER ENOUGH TRASH TO...
PERK

CHARGE!!
AH?!
HEY, YOU! WAIT!!
OOOO
YEAH!!
RSTL
RSTL
SNIFF
SNIFF
SNIFF
SNIFF
SHRUF
SHRUF
SHRUF
?!
DUN
DUUUN

A HIDDEN STASH OF PORNO MAGS?!!
AW, YEAH!
Boing!
DVD
WHAT'RE THEY DOING HERE?!
HUFF! HUFF!
PANT PANT PANT
NOT BAD, HELL-HOUND ...!
RUSTLE
NOW ALL WE NEED IS TO GATHER MORE TRASH AND...
HEY! HE RAN OFF AGAIN!!
Why won't he do what I say?!

WHERE ON EARTH COULD HE HAVE GONE...?
KYAAAAAAA?!
SHRIMP-FLAVORED POTATO CHIPS
WHOOSH
?!

WH-WHAT'S UP WITH THAT PUPPY?!
CLATTER
CLATTER
POTATO CHIPS
CHAAARGE
1 POWER
GU GU
HYAAAAA?!
KYAA!
WSH
WHOOOSH
CLATTER
POPCORN
CLATTER
2 POWER
GU GU GU GU
IYAAAA?!
HYAAAU?!
WSH
AMASH
WSH
TWING
MAX POWER

DOGGY STYLE!!
WSH
WSH
WSH
WSH
YOU'RE GOING WA OVERBOAR YOU STUP MUTT!!
WAS THIS PUPPY **ALWAYS** SUCH A PERV?!
IS HE IN HEAT?
WELL, AT LEAST THANKS TO HIM THERE'S A BUNCH MORE TRASH.
HE WON'T BE ABLE TO CLEAN ALL THIS UP ANY TIME SOON--!
SHRIMP-FLAVORED POTATO CHIPS
GLEAM
MAX

LIBIDO BREAK
CLEAN
SWEEP!!
I SHALL EXTERMINATE ALL WHO TRY TO STOP ME FROM GETTING MY TONGUE-TASTIC DUE!!
H-HE CLEANED UP ALL THAT TRASH WITH A SINGLE MOVE...?!
DOES THAT MEAN THE STRENGTH OF HIS LUST CAN OVERPOWER EVEN A DEMON?!

I'D BETTE THINK O DIFFERE PLAN O ATTACK.
BUT I CAN'T THINK STRAIGHT WITH THIS LOW BLOOD SUGAR.
CRINKLE
CRINKLE
CRINKLE

I'D BETTER EAT SOME CANDY FOR NOW...

HELL-HOUND, COME BACK FOR A MINUTE!
WHISPER
WHISPER
WE NEED TO RE-THINK OUR STRATEGY!

GYAAAA?!
POUNCE

OWWW ...!!
PANT PANT PANT
YOU CAN'T JUST POUNCE ON ME OUT OF THE BLUE LIKE...

THAT ?!
SHUDDER

H-HEY, WHY ARE YOU LICKING ME--?!
LICK
LICK
LICK
LICK
LICK
LICK
LICK
LICK
LICK
LICK
LICK
LICK

C-CUT IT OUT!!
LICK
LICK
LICK
Y...
YOU STUPID ...!
SHIVER
SHIVER
LOOK, I'LL GIVE YOU SOME-THING TO EAT! JUST LEAVE ME ALONE!!
TOSS
CHOMP
GOTCHA! DEACTI-VATE SUM-MON!!
POOF
I HEARD A WOMAN IN THE THROES OF ECSTASY, SO I CAME RUNNING!!
WHOOSH
KYAAAA!
I just can't catch a break!
GO BACK TO CLEAN-ING!!
ERR, BUT I'M ALL DONE.
ALREADY?!
WHEEZE
WHEEZE
I DON'T CARE HOW FAST YOU ARE, THERE'S NO WAY YOU COULD'VE FINISHED--

ALREADY ...?!!
GLEEEEAM
Well, that was fast.
Sure, thanks to Junji.
TROMP
TROMP

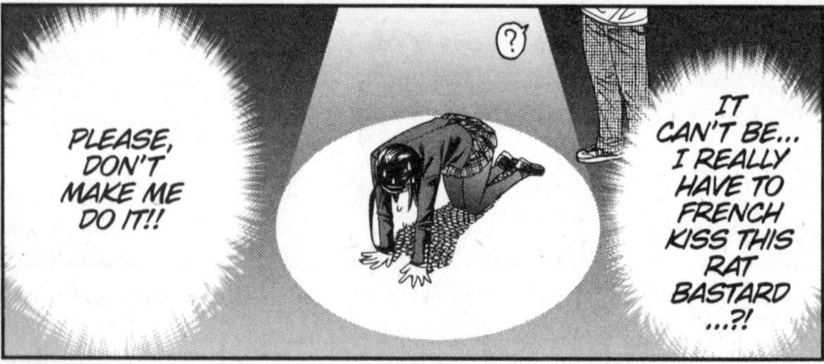
?
IT CAN'T BE... I REALLY HAVE TO FRENCH KISS THIS RAT BASTARD ...?!
PLEASE, DON'T MAKE ME DO IT!!

ALL RIGHT...
STAGGER

A PROMISE IS A PROMISE...
I'LL FRENCH KISS YOU...!!
BLUUUUSH!!

I AM CLASS PRESIDENT, AFTER ALL.
I HAVE TO BE A ROLE MODEL FOR THE OTHER STUDENTS!
THERE'S NO WAY THAT SOMEONE IN THIS POSITION CAN BREAK A PROMISE!!

PLUS...
DROP
CLACK
HE MAY BE A JERK, BUT HE DID PUT IN A LOT OF EFFORT TO CLEAN THIS PLACE UP.
SO, I...

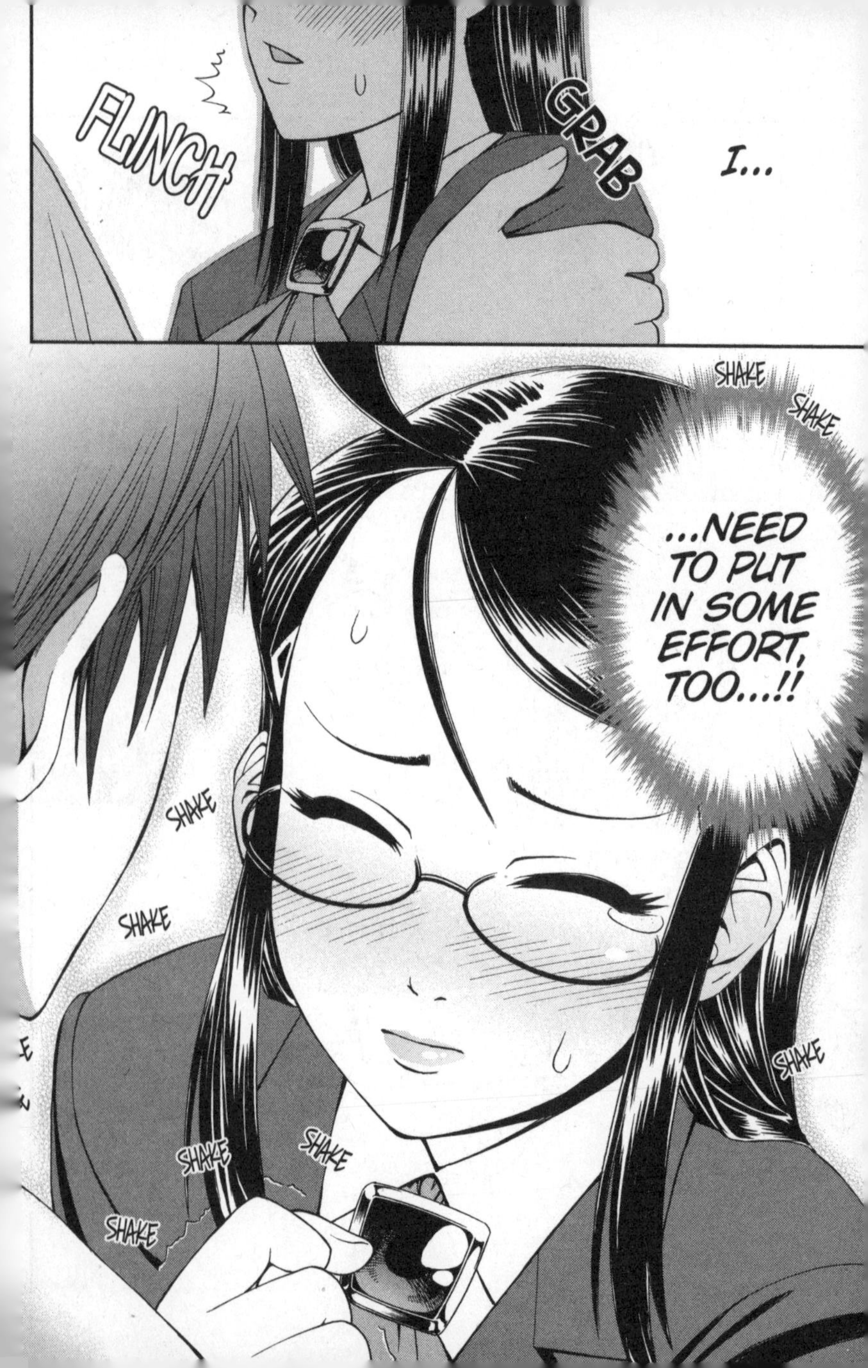
FLINCH
GRAB
I...
SHAKE
SHAKE
...NEED TO PUT IN SOME EFFORT, TOO...!!
SHAKE
SHAKE
SHAKE
SHAKE
SHAKE
SHAKE

DODGE

HEY, THERE'S SOME TRASH I DIDN'T SEE BEFORE!

WHA ...?!
AW, *MAAAN!* I DIDN'T DO A GOOD JOB CLEANING.
WELP, SO MUCH FOR THAT. GUESS I DON'T GET THAT KISS!
BUT THAT'S... AND OUR PROMISE WAS FOR--
PROMISE?

SCREW THAT! YOU'RE WAY TOO **UPTIGHT**, YOU KNOW THAT, MAKO-CHAN?
YOU NEED TO **LOOSEN UP** AND QUIT GET-TING HUNG UP ON STUFF LIKE THAT!!

JUST LET THINGS HAPPEN NATURALLY. WE COOL?
GRIN

......
NATU-RALLY !!
FLAP
JOLT
WH-WHAT THE HECK WAS THAT?
JUST ME BEING NATURAL!
LET'S GET FREAKY, MAKO-CHAN!! C'MON!
WHA ?!
HEY, DON'T RUN AWAY!
NOOO!!
AND DON'T CALL ME MAKO-CHAN!
BONK
GYA!

I NEVER WOULD'VE GUESSED...

Junji
NO BROTHERS ALLOWED!!
THAT HE'D BE THE ONE TO LET ME OUT OF THAT PROMISE.

AND HERE I THOUGHT HE WAS A HOPE-LESS RAT BASTARD.
PERHAPS... I HAVEN'T BEEN GIVING HIM ENOUGH CREDIT.

BUT HE DID GO THROUGH THE EFFORT OF RACKING UP SOME GOOD DEED POINTS.
GOOD DEED POINTS
善行値
12 Point
I SHOULD PROBABLY REWARD HIM SOMEHOW, HUH...?

W-WOULD A KISS ON THE CHEEK BE ALL RIGHT...?
I-I COULD PROBABLY MANAGE THAT MUCH... RIGHT?
HMM...

HRMM ...

SNAGGING THIS LOLLIPOP MAKO-CHAN DROPPED WAS A PRETTY SLICK MOVE...
BUT MAN, THOSE ARE SOME *DEEP* TEETH MARKS.

I WONDER IF MAKO-CHAN REALLY LIKES TO USE HER TEETH...?!
They were chattering before...
LOOKS LIKE CALLING OFF THAT KISS WAS THE RIGHT MOVE...!

WELL, ANYWAY, AS A PRESENT TO MYSELF FOR WORKING SO HARD...
I'LL TREAT MYSELF TO AN INDIRECT KISS!!
MWAAAA~!

GWO
GWO
GWO
GWO
GWO
GWO
GWO
GWO
GWO
GWO
DRIP
DRIP
DRIP

M-MAKO-CHAN?!
HMPH!
VISION
VWNN

SO, THE REASON YOU BACKED OUT OF THAT PROMISE WITHOUT BATTING AN EYE WAS BECAUSE YOU'D PLANNED TO BRING THAT LOLLIPOP HOME, HUH?
ERR ...
BLOOP
BLOOOP
YA SEE ...!
DUE TO THAT SKEEVY BEHAVIOR, THOSE GOOD DEED POINTS YOU'D FINALLY ACCUMULATED HAVE GONE BACK TO ZERO.
Down!
GOOD DEED POINTS:
善行値 0 Point

I DIDN'T MEAN ANYTHING BY IT!
IT'S JUST LIKE A GRADE-SCHOOL KID WANTING TO PLAY THE RECORDER HIS CRUSH USES IN MUSIC CLASS!!
SO CUT ME SOME SLACK!!
SUCK AWAY. IT'S NOT LIKE I EVEN TOUCHED THAT LOLLIPOP.
WHA--?!
TINK
THEN WHY WERE THERE TEETH MARKS...
ON IT?!
MY HELLHOUND FAMILIAR GOT ITS TEETH ON THAT LOLLIPOP!
Th-that was close...
SO IT'S LOADED WITH POISONOUS HELLHOUND DROOL!
NAW NAW NAW NAW

P-POI-SON?!
WHEEZE
WHEEZE
WH-WHAT'S GONNA HAPPEN TO ME?!

THAT'S THE GREAT THING.

I'M SURE YOU'LL TRANS-FORM INTO A BODY...
THUNK
THUNK
CREAK
BA-DUMP
BA-DUMP
KRIK
KRIK
...BEFITTING YOUR LUSTFUL, BEASTLY MANNER!!

HAAAUUUU-!!
AIAWOOOOOO-!!
AWOOOOOO-!!

UGH, THAT IDIOT...
AND HERE I'D ACTUALLY STARTED TO THINK BETTER OF HIM...!

AWOOOOO

THOUGH, I HAVE TO SAY...
HEH!

IT'S REALLY HARD TO STAY MAD AT HIM WHEN HE'S IN THIS STATE.
PANT
GIRLS!!
PANT
♀!!
PANT
PANT
FE-MALES!!
BUT... HE SHOULD RETURN TO NORMAL IN TWO TO THREE HOURS. MAYBE I'LL FORGIVE HIM AFTER THAT...
Maybe.

C'MON~!
NO.
C'MON! PLEASE, MAKO-CHAAAN?!
LOOK-- I SAID, "NO"!!
THOSE TWO GIRLS WHO CAME HERE BEFORE WERE YOUR FRIENDS, RIGHT?
YOU'VE GOTTA INTRODUCE ME TO THEM. ♡
YOU'D ONLY MAKE THEIR LIVES MISERABLE!

GOOD POINT! BUT AT LEAST TELL ME THEIR *NAMES*!
HEY! QUIT MAKING A SCENE ...!!
GLUMP
IT FEELS **WRONG** TO KNOW WHAT THEY LOOK LIKE BUT NOT KNOW THEIR NAMES!
I'LL DO A GOOD DEED IF YOU TELL ME!!
......

THE TALL ONE WITH THE HEADBAND IS HAYAMI SHUN-SAN.
THE SMALLER ONE WITH THE SIDE PONYTAIL IS TAMAYA KARIN-SAN.
I see, I see.
AND JUST WHAT WAS THE POINT OF LEARNING THEIR NAMES...?

WELL, I CAN'T FANTASIZE ABOUT THEM PROPERLY WITHOUT KNOWING THEIR NAMES.
MUTTER
Shun-chan and Karin-chan, huh?
HEY! WHAT DID YOU JUST SAY?!

ANYWAY! I TOLD YOU THEIR NAMES, SO LET'S GO EARN YOU SOME GOOD DEED POINTS NOW!
YOU'RE GOING TO HELP SOMEONE IN NEED!!
O-OF COURSE! OF COURSE I WILL!!
BUT YA KNOW, I DON'T THINK SOMEONE IN NEED IS JUST GONNA APPEAR OUT OF...

THIN AIR.
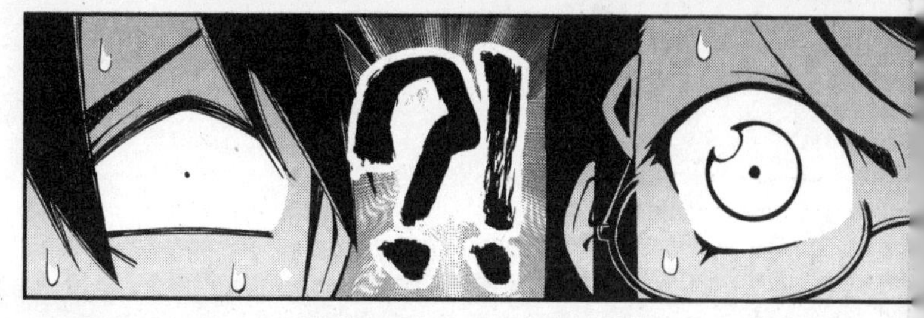
?!

HEY!! WHAT ARE YOU THINK-ING?!
LET GO OF ME! IT'S ALL OVER FOR ME!!
WHAT'S THE POINT IN *YOU* HELPING HIM, MAKO-CHAN?
THEN HOW ABOUT GIVING ME A HAND?!

Chapter 3: Become the Perfect Maid!!

Maid Café: Normal
YOU SEE, I FAILED MISERABLY AT MANAGING MY MAID CAFÉ...AND SO, NOW I'M DROWNING IN DEBT...
BUT ALL MY MAIDS QUIT ON ME...!
CLOSE
NOT THAT I CAN BLAME THEM... I DIDN'T PAY THEM FOR THREE MONTHS' WORTH OF WORK.
I LOVE MAID
Maid Café Manager
Tadokoro Fumihiko
YES, YOU WERE WRONG TO NOT PAY THEM, BUT THAT'S NO REASON TO KILL YOURSELF...
I WANTED TO SEE THIS STORE FILLED WITH CUSTOMERS, EVEN JUST ONCE...
HEY!
AND YOU! STOP GAWKING AROUND AND HELP ME OUT!!
SCAN
SCAN
......
STOP THAT!!
IT DOESN'T HAVE ENOUGH...
HUH?

...OF THE CRUCIAL INGRE-DIENT!!
?!
DU-DUUN
THIS CAFÉ IS MISSING THE MOST IMPORTANT THING!
THE THING THAT WOULD ALLOW EVEN A SMALL CAFÉ LIKE THIS TO STAND OUT AND FLOUR-ISH!!
WSH

WH-WHAT ?!
AND WHAT EXACTLY IS IT THAT MY CAFÉ LACKS, HUH?!
ELEMEN-TARY, MY DEAR WATSON !!
ORIGI-NALITY !!
SNAP

YOU NEED SOMETHING UNIQUE TO DRAW THE CUSTOMER'S ATTENTION!
YOU MUST ENSNARE YOUR CUSTOMERS BY OFFERING A SERVICE THEY CAN'T GET ANYWHERE ELSE!!
DON'T YOU AGREE THAT ORIGINALITY'S THE ONLY WAY FOR A SMALL CAFÉ TO SURVIVE...?
TWING

Y-YOU HAVE A POINT... THIS WHOLE TIME I'VE JUST BEEN IMITATING OTHER CAFÉS.

HE WAS ABLE TO REACH THE HEART OF THE PROBLEM IN A SINGLE INSTANT! WHAT AMAZING POWERS OF OBSERVATION...
WHO ON EARTH ARE YOU?!

MY APOLOGIES, GOOD SIR, FOR THE BELATED INTRODUCTION.
CLACK

I'M KNOWN THROUGHOUT THE WORLD AS...
MAID MASTER JUNJI!!
I CAN ALMOST GUARANTEE THAT NO ONE'S EVER CALLED HIM THAT...
And where'd you get those clothes, anyway?
DA-DAN

WHAT SAY YOU LEAVE THIS CAFÉ IN MY CARE?! I SWEAR THAT I'LL FILL IT TO CAPACITY WITH CUSTOMERS ...!!
WHA ?!
BOW
D-DO YOU MEAN THAT?!
COULD I LEAVE YOU IN CHARGE OF PRO-CURING THE GROCERIES, MY GOOD MAN...?
YOUR WISH IS MY COMMAND, MAID MASTER !!
WHISPER
JUST WHAT THE HECK ARE YOU TRYING TO PULL?! YOU NEED TO THINK BEFORE YOU OPEN YOUR MOUTH...!
WHISPER
WHISPER
NON, NON!
YOU WANTED ME TO PERFORM A GOOD DEED, MADEMOI-SELLE? TO THAT END...

I'M ASKING FOR YOUR SERVICES AS A MAID IN THIS FINE CAFÉ!
WH-WHY ME?!
Y-YOU WON'T ...?
O-OF COURSE I WILL! IT'D BE MY PLEASURE !!
TWITCH

MAGNI-FIQUE!
A WISE DECISION.
UGH... WHY ME...?
BUT WE'LL BE TOTALLY UNDER-STAFFED IF I'M THE ONLY ONE HERE. WE'D NEED AT LEAST ONE OR TWO MORE...
KA-CHAK
AH! THERE YOU ARE~!!

YO, CLASS PREZ~!
WE'RE BACK! ♪
HUH?! WHY ARE YOU TWO HERE IN THE HUMAN REALM?!

YOU CAN BLAME THIS LITTLE FELLA.
PANT
PANT
PANT
MAGIC
MY HELL-HOUND?!
THANKS FOR BRINGING HIM ALL THIS WAY...
XCUSEZ-MOI, SHUN-CHAN AND KARIN-CHAN!!
HE WAS RUNNING AROUND AT SCHOOL, AND WHEN WE CAUGHT HIM...
WOOF!
HE SAID, "I BELONG TO THE CLASS PRESIDENT," SO WE BROUGHT HIM HERE.
EXCEL-LENTE! WE'VE GOT A SPORTY AND A LOLI!!
WITH YOU TWO HERE, WE HAVE THE PERFECT ENSEMBLE!!
S'IL VOUS PLAIT, WOULD YOU DO US THE HONOR OF WORKING HE...
RE?!
WHOOSH
TH-CHOP
...!!
...!!
WHEEZE
WHEEZE
WRITHE
WRITHE
I APPRECI-ATE YOU BRINGING ME MY HELL-HOUND.
BUT, YOU TWO...
Why does he know our names?

HOW ARE YOUR FINALS COMING?
UH, ABOUT THAT, CLASS PREZ...
I KNOW I PROMISED THAT I WOULD HELP YOU...
BUT THAT DOESN'T MEAN I'M GOING TO JUST DO IT ALL FOR YOU.

SO, YOU TWO NEED TO GO BACK TO THE MAGIC REALM AND FOCUS ON YOUR FINALS!!
BARK
BARK
AND FOR ONE THING...
BARK
BARK
BARK
BARK
ATTENDEZ, MAKO-CHAN!
KOFF
AREN'T YOU TRYING AWFULLY HARD TO SEND THEM AWAY?!
KOFF

COULD IT BE THERE'S A CERTAIN JE NE SAI QUOIS THAT YOU DON'T WANT THEM TO KNOW ABOUT?
TWITCH
WHISPER
YOU'RE WHAT I DON'T WANT THEM TO KNOW ABOUT!!
WHISPER
WHISPER
I HAVEN'T TOLD ANYONE ABOUT HOW I SCREWED UP AND MADE THE SOUL PACT WITH YOU!!
POKE
POKE

WHISPER
POURQUOI? THEY'RE YOUR FRIENDS, AREN'T THEY? SHOULDN'T YOU BE ABLE TO TELL THEM?
WHISPER
?
WHISPER
WHISPER
IT'S BECAUSE THEY'RE MY FRIENDS THAT I CAN'T TELL THEM!!
WHISPER
WHISPER
THOSE TWO DEPEND ON ME.
ALL BECAUSE I'M THE PERFECT CLASS PRESIDENT!!
SO, IF THEY EVER FOUND OUT THAT I'D MADE A BLUNDER LIKE THIS...
IT WOULD TOTALLY BETRAY THEIR TRUST IN ME!
THAT'S WHY...I CAN NEVER TELL THEM ABOUT THIS!!
NEVER-THELESS, WE ARE STILL UNDER-STAFFED.
GULP!
WOBBLE
!!
SLUMP
SLUMP
SLUMP
SLUMP

I GUESS WE DON'T HAVE A CHOICE... ALL RIGHT. I'LL ASK THEM.
BUT THERE'LL BE HELL TO PAY IF YOU TRY ANY FUNNY BUSINESS WITH EITHER OF THEM!!
CLOSE
J'AI COMPRIS !!
<I get it!!>
AND WHAT'S WITH ALL THE FRENCH, ANYWAY ...?

WORKING PART-TIME AT A MAID CAFÉ?!
THAT SOUNDS SUPER COOL! I WONDER WHAT IT'S LIKE TO WORK IN THE HUMAN REALM!!

MERCI BEAUCOUP !!
BOW
ALL RIGHT. LET'S HURRY UP AND GET CHANGED...
SAY, DON'T YOU THINK THESE UNIFORMS ARE A BIT PLAIN?
YOU THINK SO?
BUT THERE AREN'T ANY OTHER CLOTHES ...
JUST LEAVE THAT TO ME!!
TRANSFORM
VWNN
?!

COSTUME CHANGE !!

?!
POOF
C'EST TRES JOLIE!!
WITH THOSE SKILLS, YOU CAN ACCOMPLISH ANY COSPLAY AT THE DROP OF A HAT!!
NOW, WAIT JUST A MINUTE! DON'T YOU THINK THESE SKIRTS ARE TOO SHORT?!
MAKO-CHAN... THIS IS ALL PART OF THE GOOD DEED...
ALL RIGHT, ALL RIGHT!!
ÇA Y EST!! NOW OUR STAFFING IS COM-PLETE!!
AU SUIVANT! LET'S PRACTICE YOUR CUSTOMER SERVICE!!

Normal
NOW THEN, DO IT JUST LIKE I TAUGHT YOU.
LET'S START WITH YOU, MAKO-CHAN!
YOU CAN DO IT, CLASS PREZ!!
ALL RIGHT... HERE GOES...
AHEM.
WELCOME BACK, MASTER.
HAVE YOU DECIDED ON YOUR ORDER?
PLEASE COME AGAIN, MASTER.
WHOA, CLASS PREZ~! YOU TOTALLY NAILED IT!!
CLAP
CLAP
WELL, OF COURSE. THIS *IS* JUST ANOTHER ASSIGNMENT, AFTER ALL.
CAN YOU IMAGINE THE SHAME IF I COULDN'T GET *THAT* RIGHT...

NON, NON!!
HUH?!
SIGH!
YOU'RE OBVIOUSLY JUST PRETENDING TO BE A MAID! TRULY YAWN-INDUCING!!
WHAT?!
......
HE HUMILIATED ME...!!
In front of them!
AU SUIVANT! KARIN-CHAN!!
WAVE
S-SURE THING!!
W-WELCOME BAAAA-AAA--?!
TRIP
HEY! WATCH IT!!
KA-CRAAAASH

AHHH! I'M SO SORRY!
TAMAYA-SAN... YOU'RE REALLY GOING TO HURT YOURSELF. MAYBE YOU SHOULD QUIT WHILE--
EXCEL-LENTE!!
WHA?!
IT WAS TRULY A FEAST FOR THE EYES-- A GENUINE KLUTZY MAID WHO WASN'T JUST FAKING IT!
EHEHE.
...
AU SUIVANT! SHUN-CHAN!!
AYE, AYE~!
WHASSUP, MASTER?
LAAAAAZE—
WOULD YOU TAKE THIS SERIOUSLY?!

EXCEL-
LENTE
!!
WHY
?!
Man, this uni-form's tight.
A LAZY MAID! WHY, THAT'S JUST AS DELIGHTFUL IN ITS OWN WAY!!

AND JUST WHAT'S WRONG WITH THE NORMAL WAY...?!
C'EST TERRI-BLE!!
STOMP
HAVE YOU FORGOTTEN THAT WE'RE TRYING TO GIVE THIS CAFÉ ITS OWN PERSON-ALITY?!
FLINCH

THERE'S NO POINT IN PLAYING IT BY THE BOOK!
NO POINT
W/ha ...?
DUN-DUUUN
TRY TO MAKE YOURSELF USEFUL BY AT-TRACTING SOME CUSTOM-ERS!!
ALL RIGHT, LADIES. IT'S ALMOST TIME TO OPEN SHOP! ARE BOTH OF YOU READY?!
......!!
Y-YES, SIR!!
YEP!

Maid Café: Normal
And then, after the café opened...
YOU'RE FRICKIN' KIDDING ME!!
THAT MAID JUST SPILLED WATER ALL OVER US...
STORM
STORM
AND THEN HAS THE NERVE TO SAY THERE'S NO EXTRA CHARGE!! THE HELL?!
STORM
STORM
AND THE OTHER MAID WAS JUST NAPPING THE ENTIRE TIME!
SNOOORE
I'M NEVER COMING BACK TO THIS CRAPPY PLACE AGAIN!!
I'M SORRY... THIS IS ALL BECAUSE I SPILLED WATER ON THEM...
NON, NON!
YOU'VE DONE WELL, KARIN-CHAN!!
EMPTY

THE CUSTOMER ARE THE PROBLEM
AND HERE WE TREATED THEM TO A KLUTZY MAID SLIPPING UP AND A LAZY MAID FALLING ASLEEP ON THE JOB...
THE GALL OF THOSE SWINE NOT TO APPRECIATE THE PEARLS WE OFFERED THEM!!
CLENCH
HUH? WE HAD CUSTOMERS?

HEY, THIS PLACE IS TOTALLY EMPTY.
WON'T THE MANAGER LOSE THE SHOP AT THIS RATE?
TWITCH
GWO GWO GWO GWO GWO
LEND ME YOUR SPECIAL SKILLS...
FOR THE SAKE OF THIS CAFÉ, S'IL VOUS PLAÎT?
?

NOW THAT THINGS HAVE COME TO THIS...
SMIRK
IT'S TIME TO PULL OUT ALL THE STOPS... ESPECIALLY YOU, SHUN-CHAN!

HONESTLY, WHY AM I STUCK SHILLING FOR CUSTOMERS...?
MAID CAFÉ
NORMAL
Welcome back, master!♪
Maids with different personalities are waiting for your return!
SUSHI YOJI-ROUYA
IT DOESN'T MATTER HOW MUCH PERSONALITY THE MAIDS HAVE, IF THEY DON'T HAVE SOMEONE WHO'LL WORK LIKE A NORMAL PERSON, THEY'RE NOT GOING TO KEEP ANY CUSTOMERS...!!
SUSHI

AND YET, HE JUST HAD TO GO OUT OF HIS WAY TO SCOLD ME AND EMBARRASS ME IN FRONT OF MY FELLOW STUDENTS...!!
EVEN THOUGH I'M SUCH A PERFECT CLASS PRESIDENT THAT I'M HIDING MY FAILURE FROM THEM...!!
?
RMB RMB RMB RMB RMB RMB RMB RMB RMB RMB

"HIDING" ...?
BUT...

IS IT REALLY OKAY FOR ME TO HIDE THINGS FROM THEM?
I THOUGHT I WAS DOING IT TO PROTECT THEIR TRUST IN ME...
BUT ISN'T THE VERY FACT I'M HIDING SOMETHING FROM THEM A BETRAYAL OF THAT TRUST?
WHAT SHOULD I DO...?
PARDON ME!!
Welcome back,
Maids with different pe
are waiting for your

IS MAID CAFÉ: NORMAL OVER THAT WAY?
AH, YES. IT IS.
MAID CAFÉ NORMAL
Welcome back, master!
Maids with different personalities are waiting for your return!
HEY, GUYS! SHE SAYS IT'S OVER THERE!

?!
LET'S HURRY!
AREN'T THEY HOLDING SOME INSANE EVENT ?!
I'VE NEVER EVEN HEARD OF THIS KIND OF THING BEFORE!
C'MON! ALL THE SEATS ARE GONNA FILL UP!
TROMP
TROMP
TROMP
TROMP

WH...
WHAT'S WITH THAT THRONG OF CUSTOMERS...?!

MY ORDER'S READY!
SAME HERE!
CLAAAMOR
COME CLOSER !!

3-A
TAMAYA
AS YOU DESIRE, MASTER!!
YEEEAH!
UH, SHUN-CHAN... I'M NOT SURE WE CAN STILL CALL THIS PLACE A "MAID" CAFÉ...
GYM UNI-FORMS!
CAT EARS!
WHISPER WHISPER
THERE'S NOTHING WE CAN DO! YOU-KNOW-WHO SAID WE HAD TO DO THIS OR WE WOULDN'T GET ANY CUSTOM-ERS!!
WHISPER

AND THE TRUTH IS, THESE GUYS SHOWED UP IN DROVES AFTER WE CHANGED, SO WE'VE GOTTA STICK WITH IT!!
WOOOOO!
JUST BE GRATE-FUL HE DOESN'T HAVE YOU POLE DANCING!!
MAN, DOES IT GET HOT IN THESE BUNNY GIRL SUITS...
It's all sticky.
TUG
WHOOA!
A LAZY BUNNY GIRL DOING A POLE DANCE!
YEAH!
WOO!
I'VE NEVER SEEN ANYTHING LIKE IT!
WOO!
WHOA! CAT EARS!
WOW, THOSE ARE REALLY WELL MADE!
PANT
PAANT
THEY'RE SO SOFT AND FLUFFY!
TWITCH
TWITCH
TWITCH
TWITCH

THIS IS GREAT! THIS TAIL TOTALLY SEEMS REAL!
C'MON, LET ME PET IT.
GRAB
FLINCH
HYAAAN?!
D-DON'T YANK ON IT LIKE THAT!
SHUN-CHAN USED TRANSFORMATION MAGIC, SO THIS IS A *REAL* TAIL!!
RUB RUB
WHOA! IT'S *MOVING* !!
SHUDDER
HUH? WHAT DID YOU SAY?
THEY REALLY GOT ALL THE DETAILS DOWN COLD! THIS CAFE *ROCKS* !!
SHUDDER
SHUDDER
SHUDDER
OUR AUDIENCE IS WHIPPED INTO A FRENZY... THIS IS IT!!
SMIRK
WOO!
WOOHOO!
YEAH!
LE SPECTACLE VA COMMENCER!
<It's showtime!>
TWITCH
TWITCH

WHAT YOU'RE ABOUT TO WITNESS IS AN EVENT UNIQUE TO OUR VENUE! AN EXPERIENCE YOU CAN'T GET ANYWHERE BUT HERE, FOLKS!
LET THE COSTUME CHANGE SHOW BEGIN!
FLASH
THE RULES ARE SIMPLE!
YOU'LL BE PLAYING A GAME WITH THE MAIDS!
THE WINNER GETS THE RIGHT TO CHOOSE WHAT THE MAIDS WILL WEAR NEXT!
婦警
SEXY LADY COP
ナース
SEXY NURSE
AND NO MATTER WHAT COSTUME YOU ASK FOR, OUR CAFÉ'S UNIQUE RESOURCES WILL MAKE SURE YOU GET YOUR WISH!!
"UNIQUE RESOURC-ES"?! IS HE TALKING ABOUT MY MAGIC ?!

ARE YOU INTO THE SEXY-TYPE LIKE SHUN-CHAN?! OR DO YOU PREFER THE FETISHISTIC CHARMS OF KARIN-CHAN?
IS IT JUST ME OR IS THIS GETTING CREEPY ?!
I'M SCARED ...!
YOU MASTERS WILL DECIDE WHAT THESE BEAUTIES PUT ON-- OR TAKE OFF!!
GWO
GWO
GWO
GWO
GWO
GWO
GWO
GWO
GWO
GWO

NOW, THEN!
WITHOUT FURTHER ADO, LET US...

GWAM
BE-
GIIH?!
!!

M-MAKO-CHAN?! WHAT ARE YOU DOING HERE?!

I TOLD YOU, DIDN'T I...?
HUH...?

I TOLD YOU THERE'D BE HELL TO PAY IF YOU TRY ANY FUNNY BUSINESS WITH MY FRIENDS!!
GLARE

AND WHAT'S UP WITH THIS VULGAR FARCE YOU'RE ENACTING?!
MURMUR
IS THIS PART OF THE EVENT?
MURMUR
NO MATTER HOW MUCH I SCOLD YOU FOR IT, YOUR PERSONALITY NEVER IMPROVES, AND YOU CAN'T EVEN PERFORM A SINGLE GOOD DEED!
YEAH, I KINDA ...
MURMUR
MURMUR
THE HECK?
MURMUR
YOU ALWAYS COME UP WITH THE STUPIDEST STUFF ALL BECAUSE YOU'RE IN PERVERT DREAMLAND 24/7!
YA KNOW, IT MIGHT JUST BE...
MURMUR
MURMUR
THERE ISN'T A SOUL ALIVE THAT'S FURTHER AWAY FROM BEING GOOD THAN YOU!!

JUST GROW UP ALREADY!
SHOW A LITTLE REMORSE FOR ONCE IN YOUR LIFE!!

GASP!
STUNNED

CRAP...
I GOT CAUGHT UP IN THE MOMENT AND CHEWED HIM OUT ON STAGE!!

E-EVERY-ONE'S LOOKING AT ME...!

Y...
WHAT CAN I DO TO FIX THIS...?!

YES, CLASS PREZ !!
WOOO!
?!
STARTLE

ROOOOAAARR
WHA... HUH ...?!
CLASS PREZ!
CHEW ME OUT, TOO!
WHAT THE HELL ...?!
LEC-TURE ME!
CRUSH MY SPIRIT!

ALLOW ME TO EXPLAIN! WHEN MAKO-CHAN UNLEASHED HER POTENT "CLASS PRESIDENT" AURA...
SHE WAS ABLE TO SNAP THESE MEN OUT OF THEIR LUST-DAZE, AND SIMULTA-NEOUSLY TURN THEM ON TO "CLASS PRESIDENT FETISHISM"!!
WHAT JUST HAP-PENED ...?
YEEEEAH!!

WELL, THIS CERTAINLY ISN'T WHAT I WAS EXPECTING, BUT APPARENTLY SPEAKING MY MIND WAS THE RIGHT CALL...
WOO!
WOO!
YEAH!
WOO!
SIGH...
I FEEL A BIT BAD THAT EVERYONE IN EARSHOT HEARD IT, THOUGH...

HM...?
"IN PERVERT DREAMLAND 24/7!"
"YOUR PERSONALITY NEVER IMPROVES!"
"FURTHER AWAY FROM BEING GOOD!"
"CAN'T EVEN PERFORM A SINGLE GOOD DEED!"
"ANYONE IN EARSHOT"...?

In Earshot
......
3-A TAMAYA
DAMMIT!!

After closing up shop.
I'M SORRY I LIED TO YOU...

YOU SEE, I MESSED UP MAKING THE SOUL PACT FOR MY FINAL EXAM.
BUT... I DIDN'T WANT YOU TWO TO KNOW ABOUT IT...

I WANTED TO STAY THE FLAWLESS CLASS PRESIDENT IN YOUR EYES.
SO...

FLINK
OW?!
PWUNK

WH-WHAT'S THE BIG IDEA...?!
THROB
THROB
THAT'S NOT WHAT WE WANT TO HEAR!!

WHY DID YOU HIDE IT...?!
WHY WOULDN'T YOU TELL US...?!

WELL... I DIDN'T WANT YOU TO BE DISAP-POINTED IN ME...
WOW, YOU'RE REALLY BEING THICK, AREN'T YOU?! THAT'S NOT IT AT ALL!!

SHEESH. HONESTLY, YOU'RE COMPLETELY CLUELESS WHEN IT COMES TO STUFF LIKE THIS, CLASS PREZ.
YOU'RE SERIOUSLY GONNA MAKE ME SPELL IT OUT FOR YOU?! MAN, THIS IS WEAK...
?

WHAT DO YOU ME--
HUH ?!
GRAB
WE'RE SAYING YOU CAN LEAN ON US!
AFTER ALL...

WE'RE YOUR FRIENDS !!

WH...

WHAT ARE YOU GOING ON ABOUT ?!
WHIP
YOU TWO SHOULD BE FOCUSING ON YOUR OWN FINALS!!
AAAND SHE'S BACK. THAT'S THE CLASS PREZ WE KNOW AND LOVE!!

BESIDES, WE TOTALLY KNEW ABOUT YOU MESSING UP THE SOUL-PACT ALL ALONG.
ROVER TOLD US ALL ABOUT IT.
WHAA ?!

WH-WHY DIDN'T YOU SAY SOMETHING ABOUT THAT EARLIER?!
I WANTED TO, BUT SHUN-CHAN SAID--

I TOLD HER IT WOULD BE *WAY* FUNNIER IF YOU FOUND OUT THIS WAY!
OH, FOR...

I HAVE TO SAY, THAT WAS ONE WORLD-CLASS CHEWING-OUT YOU GAVE THAT GUY.
EVEN I WAS STARTING TO FEEL BAD ABOUT IT.
THAT WOULD EXPLAIN THE LOOK ON YOUR FACE BACK THERE.
TOUDOU-SAN! I FINALLY FOUND YOU!!

YOU SEE, I HAVE A FAVOR I'D LIKE TO ASK!
?

THE MANAGER, HAVING SEEN THE AUDIENCE'S REACTION TO MAKO'S LECTURE...
CAFÉ CLASS PREZ
I ♥ CLASS PRESIDENTS
...DETERMINED THAT "CLASS PRESIDENTS ARE THE HOT TREND NOW," AND REMODELED HIS MAID CAFÉ INTO A CLASS PRESIDENT CAFÉ.

AND AT THE BEHEST OF THE MANAGER, MAKO-CHAN WAS TASKED WITH INSTRUCTING NEW "CLASS PRESIDENTS."
THE PERFECT CLASS PRESIDENTS THAT MAKO HERSELF EDUCATED WERE QUITE WELL-RECEIVED AND ATTRACTED MANY CUS-TOMERS TO THE CAFÉ.

TO THIS DAY, THE MANAGER IS LEADING A BUSY, FULFILLING LIFE.
AND WHY AM I STUCK WORKING IN THE KITCHEN?!
BECAUSE BEFORE, YOU WERE JUST MESSING AROUND AND INDULGING YOURSELF, SO YOU DIDN'T EARN A SINGLE GOOD DEED POINT!
SO I'M MAKING DAMN SURE YOU EARN AT LEAST A FEW BY VOLUNTEER-ING NOW!!
I'm not even getting paid?!
BURBLE
KA-SHRZZ
KA-SHRZZ

SORRY TO TROUBLE YOU...
Dear Toudou-san,
I'll be out volunteering today, so can I please ask you to take care of lunch?
Jun
BUT WHERE WOULD I FIND THE CERAMIC BAKING PANS?
THEY'RE IN THOSE CABINETS.
UGH... WHY ARE THEY SO HIGH UP?
SCRAPE
NYA—NI
ARE YOU SURE THEY'RE UP HERE?
I DON'T SEE THEM ANY-WHERE.
I DON'T SUPPOSE YOU'D--
MA MA M
Magical Director Mako-chan's Magical Guidance
Chapter
Transformation, Reformation, ar
the Formation of a God (Part

WHY, YOU PER-VERTED LITTLE DEVIL !!
GET BACK HERE !!

WHY DO YOU HAVE TO DO THIS EACH AND EVERY TIME?!
I DON'T HAVE A CHOICE!
IT'S NOT LIKE I *WANT* TO DO IT, EITHER!
ZOOM
THERE'S A DARK-NESS DEEP INSIDE OF ME!
THAT'S MAKING ME DO THESE THINGS!
So, it's totally not my fault!
DON'T GET ALL PSYCHO-LOGICAL ON ME!!

RUSTLE
BWAH !!
WHOA!
RUSTLE
RUSTLE
RUSTLE
HE JUMPED STRAIGHT INTO THE HEDGE!!

NOW, YOU GET YOUR BUTT BACK--
DASH

ハバーシャ
SPLAAASH
DRIP
DRIP
AAAAAH!! I-I'M SO SORRY!!
DRIP
A-ARE YOU ALL RIGHT?!
......
DRIP
D
MY SINCEREST APOLOGIES FOR GETTING YOUR CLOTHES WET...!
IT'S OKAY, REALLY ...
IT WAS MY FAULT FOR JUMPING OUT LIKE THAT.

NO! IT WAS MY FAULT FOR NOT PAYING ATTENTION!
SO I TAKE FULL RESPONSIBILITY! PLEASE ALLOW ME TO DRY YOUR CLOTHES!!
IT WON'T TAKE LONG!
I'LL DO WHAT-EVER IT TAKES!
I'LL DRY YOUR CLOTHES EVEN IF IT COSTS ME MY LIFE!!
THAT'S... A LITTLE EXTREME.
UH, OKAY.
SO, NOW WHAT DO I DO? SHE WAS APOLOGIZING SO VIGOROUSLY THAT I JUST KIND OF GOT SUCKED INTO THIS PLACE.
BUT HONESTLY, I SHOULDN'T JUST BE SITTING AROUND IDLY LIKE THIS.
THAT JERK'S STILL ON THE LOOSE, AFTER ALL.

THAT'S RIGHT. I MEAN, I CAN ALWAYS JUST USE MAGIC TO DRY MY CLOTHES.
PLUS, SINCE I HAVEN'T USED A LOT OF MAGIC RECENTLY, I SHOULD HAVE PLENTY OF MAGIC POWER TO SPARE.
I HATE TO TROUBLE HER, BUT I THINK I'LL ASK FOR MY CLOTHES BACK.
CREAK
UM, EXCUSE ME.

DRY
VWUN

WHY DON'T I JUST TAKE MY CLOTHES--
STARTLE
DRY
?!!

MAGIC ...?!
WHO IS THIS GIRL...?
U-UH...
THIS...
ISN'T WHAT IT LOOKS LIKE ...!!
P...
PLEASE ALLOW ME TO ERASE YOUR MEMORY !!
ERASE
VWRNN
WAH?! WAIT A SEC!!
I'M A MAGIC-USER, TOO!!
I SEE. SO, YOU CAME TO THE HUMAN REALM...
SWIK
SWIK
FOR YOUR FINAL EXAM, TOO, MAKO-SAN?

OH, PLEASE FORGIVE ME FOR NOT INTRODUCING MYSELF EARLIER.
MY NAME IS AMANO SERA!

BUT WHY ARE YOU DRESSED AS A SHRINE MAIDEN?
WELL, YOU SEE, I CAME TO THE HUMAN REALM WITHOUT ANY REAL PLAN.
THE PRIEST HERE WAS KIND ENOUGH TO LET ME USE ONE OF HIS ROOMS...
WHSH
SO, TO THANK HIM, I HELP OUT A LITTLE, DOING THINGS LIKE THIS.
WHSH
WHSH
WHSH
WHSH
A LITTLE ...?

BUT MY FINAL EXAM IS SO DIFFICULT, I HAVEN'T MADE ANY PROGRESS AT ALL.
WHAT DO YOU HAVE TO DO FOR YOUR FINAL, SERA-SAN?

WHY, OBVIOUSLY...
IT'S TO FIND A BAD PERSON AND SEAL HIM AWAY!!
CLENCH
SEAL AWAY?! THAT SEEMS A BIT *EXTREME*, DON'T YOU THINK...?!

BUT IT'S BEEN ROUGH TRYING TO FIND A BAD PERSON.
YEAH, I HAD A REALLY HARD TIME FINDING MY TARGET, TOO.
PEOPLE IN THE HUMAN REALM NEVER SEEM TO FIT NICELY INTO GOOD OR BAD, HUH?
I KNOW, RIGHT?!
STILL, MY GRADUATION IS RIDING ON THIS TEST, SO I KEPT SEARCHING AND FINALLY FOUND SOMEONE.

GRADUATION... THAT MUST MEAN YOU'RE A SENIOR, HUH?
YOU'RE A YEAR OLDER THAN I AM, THEN.
SO, THE PERSON YOU FOUND FOR YOUR FINAL. WHAT'S HE LIKE?
UM...
WELL, HIS NAME IS ONODERA JUNJI AND...
WAH HA HA HA!
UUGH...
FLINCH

WHAT'S THE MATTER ...?
I'M SORRY! BUT CAN WE PLEASE TALK ABOUT SOMETHING ELSE?
AH! FORGIVE ME!!
I JUST GOT CARRIED AWAY SINCE I NEVER EXPECTED I COULD TALK WITH ANYONE IN THE HUMAN REALM ABOUT MY TEST...!
GLOOOOOM

SERA-SAN, MAKE SURE YOU'RE EXTRA CAREFUL WHEN YOU PERFORM YOUR PACT TO SEAL AWAY YOUR PERSON, OKAY?
UM, OKAY ...?

I'LL DO MY BEST!!

I'LL WORK HARD TO COMPLETE THE TEST, THEN GRADUATE...
AND THEN WORK TO HELP MAKE THE WORLD A BETTER PLACE.
THAT'S BEEN MY DREAM EVER SINCE I WAS A LITTLE KID.

SERA-SAN...
HER EYES ARE SO BRIGHT AND HOPEFUL, GAZING STRAIGHT AT HER DREAMS...

THAT'S RIGHT... I HAVE A DREAM OF MY OWN. I'VE GOT TO KEEP AT IT, TOO.
I'M SURE I CAN MAKE THAT IDIOT TURN OVER A NEW LEAF!!

SERA-SAN. AS A FELLOW FINAL EXAM-TAKER, LET ME LEND YOU A HAND.
YOU MEAN IT? WELL, IF YOU SPOT A GOOD BAD GUY, LET ME KNOW!
A BAD GUY, HUH? WHY DO I GET THE FEELING I WON'T HAVE TO LOOK TOO FAR...?
PHEW! COAST SHOULD BE CLEAR NOW.
RUSTLE
RUSTLE
RUSTLE
RUSTLE
RUSTLE
THAT WAS A PRETTY SLICK FAKE OUT, MAKING IT LOOK LIKE I RAN AWAY. BY NOW, MAKO-CHAN'S PROBABLY HALFWAY TO...

RIGHT HERE ?!!!
!!
HEY !!
CLICK
Sera-Vision
H-HOW IS THIS POSSIBLE?! IT'S LIKE HIS AURA IS A MASS OF PURE EVIL?!
?
I-I'VE NEVER SEEN THIS MUCH EVIL BEFORE IN MY ENTIRE LIFE...!!
GWOOOOOOO
MAKO-SAN, STAND BACK!
I'M GOING TO SEAL THIS BAD GUY AWAY!!
W-WAIT! HE'S THE ONE I MADE THE PACT WITH!!
I'LL FAIL IF YOU SEAL HIM AWAY--!
WHSH

SAVE ME, SHRINE MAIDEN!!
EXORCISE THAT EVIL WITCH!!
?!
WHAT ARE YOU DOING, YOU IDIOT?!
GLOMP
HOW STUPID ARE YOU?!
CAN'T YOU EVEN TELL WHICH OF US IS TRYING TO HELP YOU?!
YOU'RE THE ONE WHO'S ALWAYS TRYING TO HURT ME!!
YANK
YANK
YANK
DWAH?!
YOINK

SHWUMP
!!

?!!

WH-WHAT INDECENT BEHAV-IOR...
QUIVER
QUIVER
QUIVER
QUIVER
AND WHAT AN EXTRAOR-DINARY AURA OF EVIL...!

AS AN ASPIRING ANGEL, I CAN'T ALLOW YOU TO TURN A BLIND EYE TO THIS!!
RAWR!

WHA--?!

GRAB

MY NAME IS AMANO SERA, ALSO KNOWN AS ANGEL-IN-TRAINING SERAPHIEL!
!!
IN ORDER TO PASS MY TEST TO BECOME A FULL-FLEDGED ANGEL...
I PASS JUDGMENT UPON THEE, WICKED ONODERA JUNJI, AND BANISH THEE TO THE DEMON ZONE!!

A-
AN
ANGEL
...
SERA-
SAN
IS AN
ANGEL
...?!
......?!
FLAP
FLOOF
SAY
YOUR
PRAYERS
!!
KIIIN
?!
IS SHE
SERIOUSLY
PLANNING
ON USING
MAGIC
RIGHT
HERE?!

CRAP!!
BARRIER
VWNN
BARRIER
BI-KII!!
GREAT WALL!!
BARRIER
GA-CHIIIN
THIS IS THE STRONGEST DEFENSIVE SPELL I KNOW!
NO MATTER WHAT SHE THROWS AT US, THIS ULTRA-HARD BARRIER CAN TAKE IT...!
Doesn't grasp the situation.

SEALED CITADEL!!
SEALED
BARRIER
THOON

WHA--?!
Brain shut down.
SHE SEALED US, BARRIER AND ALL?!

HOW IS THAT FAIR?!
SWOOP

RUUUUMBLE
I SUCCEEDED IN SEALING AWAY THE WICKED ONE...
MY FINAL EXAM IS COMPLETE ...!!

MY FINAL EXAM IS COMPLETE ...?
HAH!
I DID IT, MAKO-SAN!!
I FINALLY PASSED MY...
WHIP

FINAL.
AHHH?! MAKO-SAN!!!

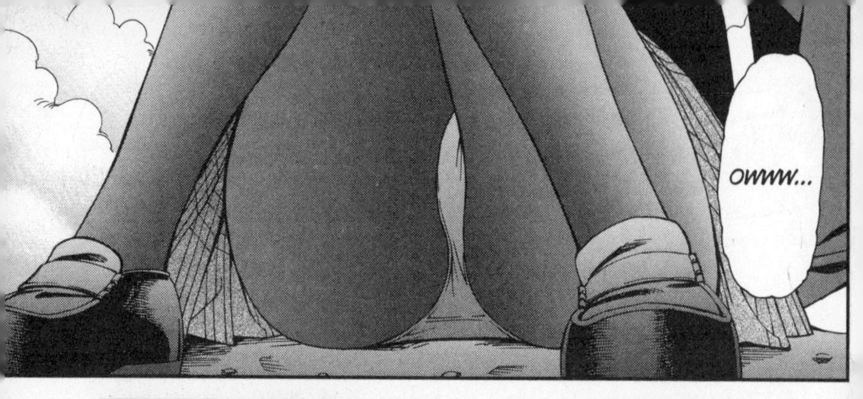
OWWW...

ANGEL MAGIC IS CRAZY STRONG.
......
BUT MORE IMPOR-TANTLY...

WHERE ARE WE...?

IS THIS THE DEMON ZONE...?
DID I GET SEALED HERE ALONG WITH THAT IDIOT...?
CRUMBLE
UNGH ...
CRUMBLE

I HAD NO IDEA ANGELS ACTUALLY EXISTED ...
BUT WHY WOULD AN ANGEL DO THIS...?
YOU REALLY HAVE TO ASK, AFTER WHAT YOU DID?!

I'M ONLY EXPLAINING THIS ONCE, SO LISTEN UP, OKAY? ANGELS ARE MAGICAL BEINGS THAT LIVE IN HEAVEN.
THEY MERCILESSLY EXTERMINATE ENEMIES OF GOD AND ANYONE THEY CONSIDER EVIL.
THINK OF THEM AS THE HOLY ARM OF JUSTICE.

YOU PULLED QUITE THE STUNT ON THAT ANGEL...
URK!
HONESTLY, IF SHE'D TAKEN YOU APART ATOM BY ATOM, I WOULDN'T HAVE BLINKED.

FROM WHAT I'VE SEEN OF HER, I'M PRETTY SURE SHE'LL COME BACK TO SAVE ME...
AFTER ALL, SHE *DID* SEAL ME HERE ALONG WITH YOU.
ANYWAY, LET'S GET MOVING.
THIS SEEMS LIKE A DANGEROUS PLACE TO STICK AROUND--
THROB

GAAH ...!!
?!

WHAT'S THE MATTER, MAKO-CHAN?
IT LOOKS LIKE...I TWISTED MY ANKLE.

ARE YOU ALL RIGHT? CAN YOU WALK?
......

THEN SADDLE UP.
RIDE ON
WHA ...?!
YOUR FOOT HURTS TOO MUCH FOR YOU TO WALK, RIGHT? THEN THERE'S ONLY ONE OPTION.

YOU'RE JUST DOING THIS FOR PERVERTED REASONS, AREN'T YOU?
DON'T WORRY.

EVEN I WOULDN'T DARE TO TRY ANY-THING WHEN YOU'RE HURT, MAKO-CHAN.

AFTER ALL, THIS WHOLE MESS IS REALLY MY FAULT.
LET ME PROVE TO YOU THAT I'M NOT ALL RAT BASTARD.

W-WELL, I SUP-POSE I CAN ALLOW IT...
HEH!

WHOAAAAAA?!!
NNRRUURRRR!
TROMP
TROMP
TROMP
TROMP
TROMP
TROMP
TROMP
TROMP
TROMP
TROMP
TROMP
NRRUR!
M-MAKO-CHAN!! CAN'T YOU USE MAGIC TO TAKE CARE OF THAT?!
I CAN'T! I NEED TO SAVE UP MY MAGIC!
YOU'RE JUST GOING TO HAVE TO OUTRUN IT!!
WELL, WHY DIDN'T I THINK OF THAT?!

WH-WHAT THE HELL IS THAT THING?!
CRUNCH
CRUNCH
QUIET!
WHEEZE
WHEEZE
DAMMIT! I DIDN'T EVEN GET TO FEEL HER BOOBS AGAINST MY BACK!!
CAUTIOUS AS EVER, HUH, MAKO-CHAN...
AND HERE I FIGURED YOU'D BE TOO EMBARRASSED TO LET ME CARRY YOU...
......

OF COURSE I'M EMBARRASSED!!
BLUUUUUSH

I-IT'S NOT LIKE I'M HAPPY TO BE CARRIED BY A JERK LIKE THIS...
WOBBLE WOBBLE

SQUEEZE
I CAN'T BELIEVE I HAVE TO HOLD ONTO HIM AND LET HIM TOUCH MY LEGS...

STUB
WHOA!
WAH?!
STUMBLE

LIGHT SQUEEZE

?!
Did something small and soft just touch me...?
TH-THAT'S IT! I CAN'T TAKE ANY MORE!!

L-LET'S TAKE A BREAK AND REST FOR A BIT!
JUST PUT ME DOWN!
YES, MA'AM.
A-AT LEAST NOW I CAN RELAX FOR A...
SIGH...
WRIGGLE

GROPE
FLINCH
HYAA?!
YOU DON'T WASTE ANY TIME, DO YOU, YOU JERK!!
GA-WHAM!!
WH-WHAT'S THE BIG IDEA?!
DON'T GIVE ME THAT! YOU TOUCHED MY BUTT AND YOU KNOW IT!!
I DID NO SUCH THING!!
BOTH MY HANDS ARE RIGHT HERE HOLDING YOUR LEGS!!
G-GOOD POINT.
TH-THEN, IF IT WASN'T YOU...?
TWITCH
STROKE
STROKE
STROKE
STROKE
STROKE
STROKE

HYA-AAA?!
FLINCH
FLINCH
FLINCH
S-SOME-THING'S...
GROPE
GROPE
GROPE
GROPE
GROPE
SOME-THING'S UNDER-NEATH ME!!
WHA-AAAA?!
SLITHER
SLITHER
TH-THIS IS SO GROSS!!
NOODLE
NOODLE
NOODLE
DON'T THRASH AROUND LIKE THAT, MAKO-CHAN!!
WRIG
WRIG
WRIG
WRIG
WRIG
I-IT'S UNDER MY CLOTH-ES!!
SLORP
WHA--?!

HEY! STOOOP!!
DON'T LET GO OF ME!!
TUG
TUG
TUG
TUG
TUG
TUG
TUG
TUG
AH?!
SLIP

OOF!
FWUMP

?!
WHA?
WHA?
WHA?

WHAAAAA?!
うじゅる
WRIGGLE
うじゅる
WRIGGLE
うじゅる
WRIGGLE
うじゅる
WRIGGLE

WH- WHAT'S WITH THESE TENTACLES?!
THEY'RE COMING OUT OF ME?!
うじゅる
WRIGGLE
うじゅる
WRIGGLE
うじゅる
WRIGGLE
うじゅる
WRIGGLE
M- MAKO-CHAN!!
ST- STAY BACK!!
RECOIL

AHHH!! CRUMBS!!
I'M TOO LATE!!!
ARE YOU ALL RIGHT, MAKO-SAN?!
FLAAP
SERA-SAN!!
DO YOU KNOW WHAT'S GOING ON HERE?!
YES! THE EVIL AURA EMANATING FROM JUNJI-SAN WAS SO STRONG...
THAT I DID SOME RESEARCH ON HIS SOUL!
AND WHAT I LEARNED WAS...

THE SOUL OF ZIHG ZAHGGER THE KING OF DEVILS, IS SEALED...
INSIDE JUNJI-SAN'S BODY!!

THE SOUL OF...
THE KING OF DEVILS ...?!

MAMAMA
TAMAYA KARIN
MAGIC
STAMINA
LUCK
SPIRIT
INTELLIGENCE
STATUS
Magic: 4 Stamina: 1 Spirit: 1 Intelligence: 3 Luck: 2
Along with Shun, she is one of Mako's close friends. Her personality is more reserved and she's a scaredy-cat. She never does anything without Mako and Shun. She's a bit slow, a klutz, and trips at every possible opportunity. Her grades tend to suffer due to all of her misfortune, and she often has Mako help her study.
The fact that she triggers explosion magic whenever she receives a strong impact causes problems for everyone around her. Paired with her natural klutziness, this means she leaves a trail of craters wherever she goes. These explosions occur because she has preter-naturally high fire magic, much to her dismay.
As a result, she wears a custom-made uniform made from fire-rat fur. It was made a little on the large size so she could grow into it, but she hasn't grown at all and it's still baggy on her even now in her senior year.
TAMAYA KARIN
★ BIRTHDAY
February 29 (Leap Day)
★ THREE SIZES
69-53-71 (AAA cup)
★ BLOOD TYPE
AB
★ LIKES
Sweets
★ DISLIKES
Stairs, running
★ HOBBY
Making sweets (though she's never been successful at it)
★ SPECIALTY
Exploding
★ BEST SUBJECT
None
★ WORST SUBJECT
Any subject that requires physical movement
★ MAGIC ELEMENT
Fire
MP 1100
TAMAYA KARIN

ZIHG ZAHGGER, THE KING OF DEVILS, IS RENOWNED FOR UNIFYING HELL UNDER A SINGLE BANNER.
HE'S THE LEGENDARY BEING WHO LAUNCHED A FULL-OUT WAR AGAINST THE ANGELS THAT SPANNED COUNTLESS MILLENNIA.

AND AFTER THE FIERCE BATTLE HAD RUN ITS COURSE, THE KING OF DEVILS WAS BESTED BY THE ANGELS WHO SEALED HIM AWAY...
SEAL
DOWN IN THE DEEPEST LAYER OF THE DEMON ZONE.

HOWEVER, THE KING O DEVILS WA CRAFTY, AN BEFORE HE W COMPLETEL SEALED AWA HE *SPLIT O* PART OF HI SOUL...
USED IT TO POSSESS AN UNBORN HUMAN BABY, THEN FELL INTO A DEEP SLUMBER.

JUNJI-SAN, THE SOUL OF THE KING OF DEVILS...
LIES SLEEPING *WITHIN* YOUR BODY!!
MA MAMA
agical Director Mako-chan's
agical Guidance
Chapter 5: Transformation, Reformation, and the Formation of a God (Part 2)

TH-THE SOUL OF THE KING OF DEVILS IS...
IN THIS RAT BASTARD'S BODY...?

ALAS, THE FACT THAT HIS TENTACLES HAVE MATE-RIALIZED MEANS...
WHA ?!
THAT THE KING OF DEVILS IS ON THE VERGE OF BEING REBORN! WE'RE IN TERRIBLE DANGER!!
AND JUST WHAT...
AM I SUP-POSED TO DO ABOUT THAT, EXACTLY ?!

LIBIDO, THAT IS TO SAY SEXUAL DESIRE, IS THE SOURCE OF THE DEVIL KING'S POWER!
SO, WHAT YOU NEED TO DO IS CALM DOWN...
CLOP
AND RESTRAIN YOUR LIBIDO!!

AS LONG AS YOU'RE CAREFUL ABOUT KEEPING YOUR DESIRES IN CHECK, THE KING OF DEVILS WILL REMAIN ASLEE--
KYAAAA?!
WHOOSH
Gust from Sera flapping her wings.
BA-DUMP

AHHH! NOW, WAIT! JUST WAIT A SEC!!
BA-DUMP
BA-DUMP
BA-DUMP
BA-DUMP
THAT DIDN'T COUNT! LET'S GET A DO-OVER! PLEASE!!
GWO GWO GWO GWO GWO GWO GWO GWO GWO GWO

!!
DWOON

WHAT'S THAT ...?!

GWROOO

GOSH DARN IT...!!

ZIGH ZAHGGER, THE KING OF DEVILS, AWAKENS!!

HEH ...

GROOO
!!

TREMBLE
WH-WHAT OVER-WHELMING MAGIC POWER...!! IT'S LIKE I'M IN A STORM!!
UGH!
SO, THIS IS THE LEGENDARY KING OF DEVILS...!!
TREMBLE
NH!
TREMBLE

IS IT YOU WHO STIRRED ME FROM MY LONG SLUMBER, FAIR MAIDENS?
A MAGIC-USER...
AND, DO MY EYES DECEIVE? A MEMBER OF THE ACCURSED ANGEL TRIBE THAT SEALED ME AWAY?

YOU HAVE MY THANKS!
SMIRK

DAM-MIT ...!
FLAP

SWOOSH
SERA-SAN?!
BEFORE THAT HAP-PENS...
I'LL SEAL HIM AWAY IN AN EVEN DEEPER DEMON ZONE!
SIMPLY SEALING AWAY THE DEVIL KING WON'T BE ENOUGH TO KEEP HIM HERE IN THE DEMON ZONE!
HE'LL WIND UP MAKING HIS WAY TO THE OUTSIDE WORLD!!
A-A BATTLE BETWEEN AN ANGEL AND THE KING OF DEVILS?!
IT'S LIKE A MYTH OR A RELIGIOUS TEXT IS UNFURLING BEFORE MY EYES...!!
HMPH.
WRIG
WRIG
WRIG
WRIG

SWUFF
?!
HEY! WHAT'S GOING ON?!
T-TENTACLES?!
WRAP
HYAU!
SLITHER
SLITHER
N-NO, PLEASE! ANY-WHERE BUT THERE...!
SLITHER
NYAAAA!
PA-YOIIING

WH- WHAT ARE YOU GOING TO DO TO ME?!
うじゅる
WRIGGLE
SLORP
SLORP
RUB
RUB
STOOOOOP!
WRIGGLE
うじゅる
WRIGGLE
うじゅる
電
ELECTRICITY
VRNN
BA-ZZRRT
KYA?!
HMPH.

MAKO-SAN!
......
WHAT'S WRONG, YOUNG LADY? DO YOU WISH TO TAKE HER PLACE AS MY PLAYTHING?
AS IF!!

NO, I'M DISGUSTED!!
YOU'RE THE LEGENDARY KING OF DEVILS THAT UNIFIED ALL OF HELL, AREN'T YOU?!
RAWR!
IS IT REALLY FITTING FOR SUCH A GREAT KING...
TO MOLEST INNOCENT GIRLS WITH HIS TENTACLES?!

TOK
WHY WOULD IT BE UNFITTING?
HUH?!
I HAVE BEEN ROUSED FROM MY SLUMBER...
SNAP

BY A BESPECTACLED MAGICAL-GIRL CLASS PRESIDENT IN BLACK TIGHTS...
AND AN UNEXPECTEDLY WELL-ENDOWED LOLI ANGEL!!
IT IS ONLY COMMON COURTESY THAT I SHOW MY GRATITUDE WITH ALL OF MY BODY, ALL OF MY SOUL, AND ALL OF MY TENTACLES!!
WAGGLE
WAGGLE
WAGGLE
HE...
HE'S A COMPLETE AND UTTER SEXUAL DEVIANT!
HE'S THE KING OF ALL DEVILS... AND A PRETTY BOY TO BOOT...!!
BUT INSIDE, HE'S NO DIFFERENT FROM JUNJI!!
YOU SEE, THIS IS WHAT MAKES THE KING OF DEVILS SO TERRIFYING!!
SERA-SAN?!

THE DEVIL KING'S HAREM
AFTER ALL, THE ENTIRE REASON THAT THE DEVIL KING UNIFIED HELL...
WAS TO CREATE A HAREM OF ALL THE MOST BEAUTIFUL WOMEN IN HELL!!
SERIOUSLY ?!

SIMILARLY, THE ENTIRE REASON BEHIND HIS WAR WITH THE ANGELS...
WAS ALLEGEDLY BECAUSE HE ASKED THEM FOR SOME ANGELS TO ADD TO HIS HAREM.
Just gimme two or three!
Go to Hell!!
THAT'S THE REASON ?!
WELL, THAT EXPLAINS HIS NOTORIETY !!

FOOLISH MAIDENS... ISN'T IT OBVIOUS?
TOK
SINCE I WAS BORN INTO THIS WORLD WITH FREE WILL...
GAINING WHAT I DESIRE IS MY BIRTH-RIGHT!!
IN OTHER WORDS, ALL WOMEN IN THIS WORLD BELONG TO ME!!
SMIRK
HOW EXACTLY DOES THAT FOLLOW ?!

FIRST, I'LL HEAD TO HEAVEN TO EXACT MY REVENGE!
NEXT, I'LL CONQUER THE HUMAN REALM WITHOUT BREAKING A SWEAT...
FINALLY, I'LL HEAD TO THE MAGIC REALM AND CLAIM THE WITCHES FOR MY OWN!!

AFTER-WARDS, I'LL RETURN TO HELL...
RUUUMBLE
?!
RUUUMBLE
AND GATHER ALL THE BEAUTIFUL WOMEN FROM EVERY REALM...

AND THEN ...!!
THROOM

LIBIDO'S EDEN
I SHALL ERECT MY PARADISE: LIBIDO'S EDEN!!
WHERE I SHALL ENJOY A SPLENDID LIFE WITH BEAUTIFUL WOMEN AT MY BECK AND CALL!!
TH-THIS DOUCHE-BAG IS WAY TOO DANGER-OUS!!
IF WE LET A DICKHEAD LIKE HIM HAVE HIS WAY...
IT'LL SPELL DISASTER FOR ALL THE WOMEN IN THE UNIVERSE !!
BUT... HOW CAN WE STOP HIM...?
FLAP

M-MAKO-SAN! YOU MUST RUN TO SAFETY!
I SHALL SEAL THE KING OF DEVILS AWAY!
WHA ?!

WHAT ARE YOU SAYING?! YOU SERIOUSLY THINK YOU CAN TAKE ON SOME-ONE THAT POWERFUL ALL BY YOURSELF ?!
B-BUT...
I MAY JUST BE AN ANGEL IN TRAINING, BUT I STILL HAVE MY PRIDE!
SHAKE
I CAN'T JUST RUN FROM EVIL LIKE THIS!
SHAKE
SHAKE

E-EVEN IF I CAN'T SEAL HIM AWAY...
I'LL AT LEAST DISTRACT HIM LONG ENOUGH FOR YOU TO ESCAPE!!

NOPE... EVEN THAT ISN'T POSSIBLE.
DU-DUUN
WHAA ?!

I HURT MY ANKLE, YOU SEE.
THROB
THERE'S NO WAY I CAN OUTRUN THE KING OF DEVILS IN THIS CONDITION.
OH NO ...!
BESIDES ...

I'M NOT ONE TO GIVE UP ONCE I'VE STARTED SOME-THING.
IF I RUN AWAY FROM THE KING OF DEVILS...
IT'LL BE THE SAME AS GIVING UP ON TURNING JUNJI INTO A DECENT GUY.

BUT... THE KING OF DEVILS POSSESSES UNFATHOMABLE MAGIC POWER...!
King of devils, waits patiently while the girls have a heart-to-heart.
IT'LL BE ALL RIGHT !!
CLASP
EVEN IF NEITHER OF US CAN DO IT ALONE...
BA-DUMP
IF WE WORK *TOGETHER*, I'M SURE WE'LL SUCCEED!

SO, PLEASE, SERA-SAN...
LEND ME YOUR STRENGTH !!

MAKO ...
ONEE-SAMA ...!!
BLUSH

SO, SERA-SAN.
AH!
WE CAN'T SEAL THE DEVIL AWAY, BUT IS THERE ANY WAY WE CAN BRING THE JERK BACK TO HIS NORMAL STUPID SELF?

HMM... WELL...
THIS IS JUST HYPOTHETICALLY SPEAKING, BUT IF WE'RE ABLE TO GET JUNJI-SAN'S SOUL TO EMERGE...
Change!
WE MIGHT JUST BE ABLE TO PUSH THE DEVIL KING'S SOUL BACK INTO JUNJI-SAN'S BODY!

OF COURSE, WE'D NEED TO AROUSE HIS SOUL WITH SOME KIND OF STRONG FORCE...
I SEE...

......!

I'VE GOT AN IDEA...!
HUH?
TOK
LEAVING ME IN SUSPENSE CAN BE PRETTY EXCITING AND ALL...
BUT DRAW IT OUT TOO MUCH AND IT KILLS THE MOOD...!
POKE
POKE
WOULDN'T YOU SAY IT'S ABOUT TIME WE HAD OUR *FUN*, YOUNG LADIES...?!
SERA-SAN... YOU DRAW HIS ATTENTION FROM THE AIR!
YOU'VE GOT IT, ONEE-SAMA!
"Onee-sama"?
OH, AND ONE MORE THING...
VNN
BROOM
...I APOLOGIZE IN ADVANCE.
?
POOF

BWOOSH
SO, THEY SPLIT UP.
AN OBVIOUS FEINT...
I'M SORRY, SERA-SAN!
KIIIIN
HUH ...?
TRANSFORM
VWNN
KYAAAAA?!
ONEE-SAMA ?!
POOF

!!
AN ANGEL MAID?! EVEN I HAVE NEVER BEHELD SUCH A WONDER!!
WRAP
STOOOOOP!
Not the tenta-cles again!
!!
GWOOOSH
NOW'S MY CHANCE!!

A SNEAK ATTACK? I THINK NOT.
VRNN
EXPLOSION
AH?!
FWOOM
DAMMIT...!
THIS STUPID RAT BAS-TARD...
WOBBLE
JUST HAS TO MAKE EVERY-THING DIFFICULT !!
YOU STUPID...
SKREE
PANG
NNH!

YOU STUPID PUSH-OVER!!
GRR!
WHAT KIND OF WEAKLING LETS HIS BODY GET TAKEN OVER BY THE KING OF DEVILS?!
LIGHT
VWNN
LUNGE
!!
LIGHT
UNTIL I'VE REFORMED YOU INTO...
A FINE, UPSTANDING CITIZEN...
FLASH

I PROMISE...
I WON'T ABANDON YOU...!

I SEE... THE RITE OF THE SOUL PACT, EH?

I TAKE IT YOU WERE ATTEMPTING TO AWAKEN THAT FOOL'S SOUL WITH THAT LITTLE STUNT?

I WOULDN'T HOLD MY BREATH IF I WERE--
WIPE

YOU SAW THE SACRIFICE I MADE FOR YOU.
SO HURRY AND WAKE UP...
IDIOT !!

ONEESAMA... HEARING HER SPEAK SO PASSIONATELY MAKES ME...
OH, SERA... SUCH THOUGHTS AT A TIME LIKE THIS...
BA-DUMP
TWITCH

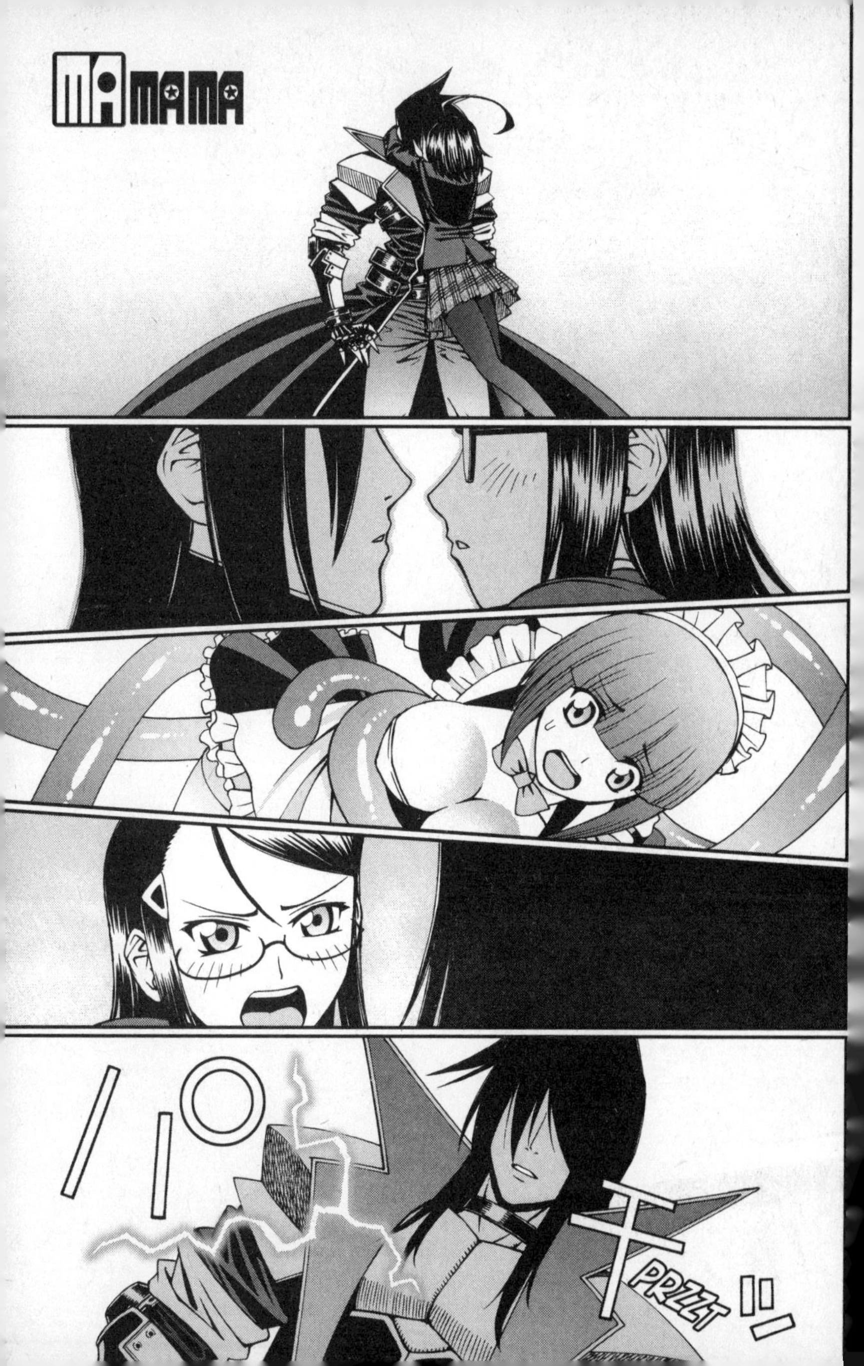
MA MAMA
PRZZT

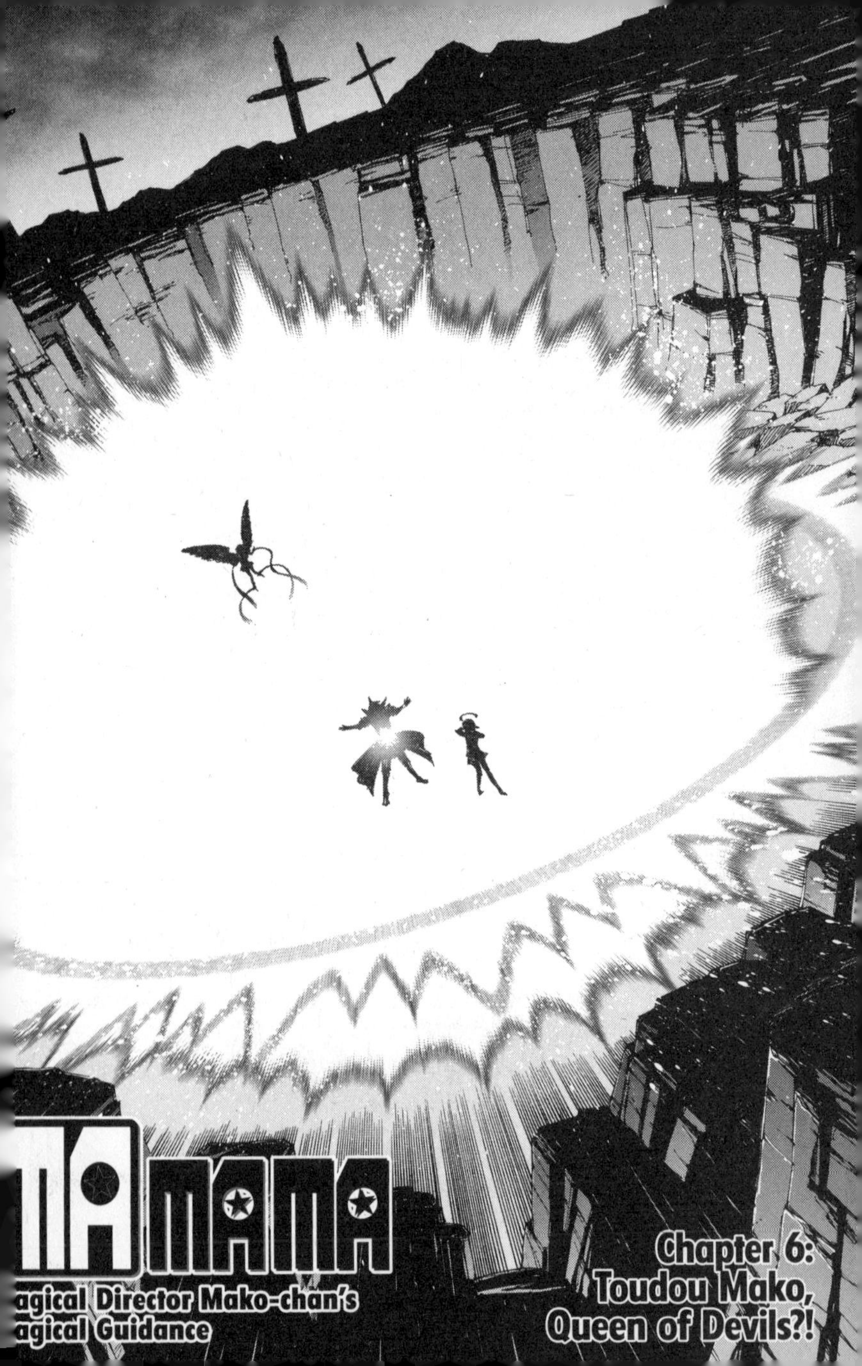
MA MAMA
agical Director Mako-chan's
agical Guidance
Chapter 6:
Toudou Mako,
Queen of Devils?!

ZUOO
......!!

ARE YOU...
BACK TO NORMAL ...?

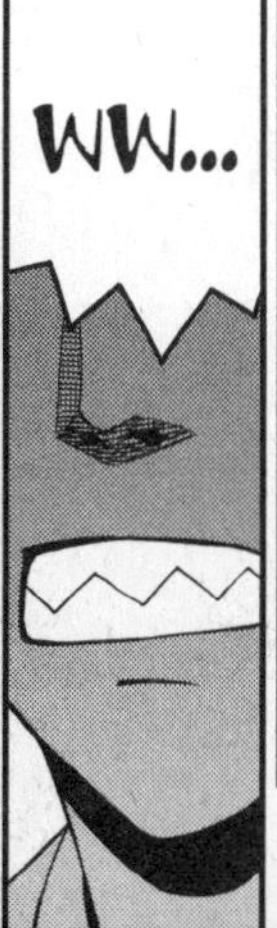

WW...

WWWWWWW.
FLINCH

WWWWHOA!
THANK YOU, MAKO-CHAN!!
!!
SPROING

I SAW THE WHOLE THING! HOW YOU KISSED THAT BASTARD FOR MY SAKE!!
THAT MUST HAVE BEEN SO HARD ON YOU! I KNOW YOU DIDN'T WANT TO DO IT!!
SO, KISS ME NOW TO GET THE TASTE OUT OF YOUR MOUTH!!
MMM~!

FOR CRYING OUT LOUD! YEAH, YOU'RE 100% BACK TO YOUR NORMAL, AWFUL SELF, ALL RIGHT...!
ARE YOU ALL RIGHT, ONEE-SAMA?!
SERA-SAN.
FLAP

IT'S ALL RIGHT. WE APPEAR TO HAVE BEEN SUCCESS-FUL.
SO WHAT SAY WE RETURN BACK TO OUR WORLD?
YES, OF COURSE... BUT...
BEFORE WE GO, PLEASE RETURN MY CLOTHES TO NORMAL!
WAAH!
R-RIGHT! IF YOU STAY LIKE THAT, THE IDIOT MIGHT TRY TO PULL SOMETHING STUPID AGAIN...
WOOO ?!
AHH!! ALREADY ?!!

HEY!! YOU KEEP AWAY FROM SERA-SAN!!
STAGGER
I ONLY HAD HER WEAR THIS TO DISTRACT THE DEVIL KING!
IT WASN'T DONE FOR YOUR...

PLEA-SURE...
GRAB
HUH ...?!
WH-WHAT ARE YOU DOING?! H-HEY --?!
SQUEEZE
UH!
NGH ...!

WHAT ARE YOU TRYING TO...
POP
GLARE

THE HELL --?!
SMIRK

?!!
ZU-BLORP

KOFF!
KOFF!
UN!
NNH!
WHAT THE HELL JUST HAP-PENED?!
MN?!

GULP!

WH...
WHAT DID I JUST SWALLOW ...?!

THOON

THAT'S THE MAGICAL ENERGY OF THE KING OF DEVILS?!
NO... CAN IT BE...?!
MAKO-CHAN --?!

POOF

POP

BOING

SMILE

HMPH... AS I SUSPECTED THE MAGIC-USER'S BOD IS MUCH EASIER TO OPERATE!
TRULY, A FITTING VESSEL TO HOUSE THE KING OF DEVILS!!
DU-DUUN
MAKO-CHAN GOT POSSES-SED BY THE DEVIL KING?!
THE WAY YOU'RE DRESSED IS TOO STIMULATING FOR ME, ONEESAMA!!

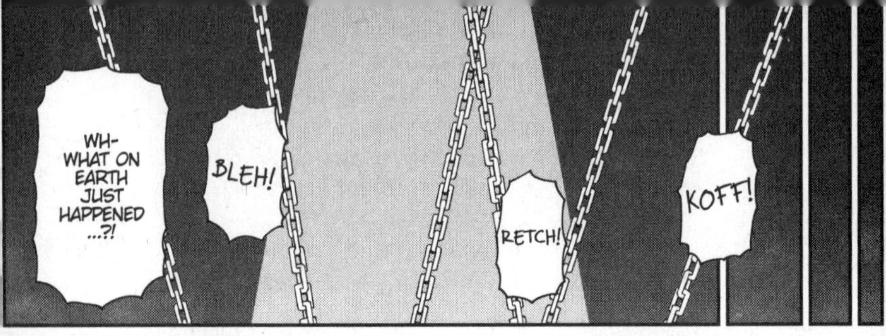
KOFF!
RETCH!
BLEH!
WH-WHAT ON EARTH JUST HAPPENED ...?!

WAIT... WHAT THE--?!
WH-WHY AM I IN CHAINS ?!
JANGLE
AND MORE IMPOR-TANTLY...

WH-WHERE AM I...?
THIS IS THE WORLD OF YOUR MIND, YOUNG LADY.
?!
I KNOW THAT VOICE ...!!

NO WAY...THE KING OF DEVILS?!
WHAT ARE YOU DOING IN HERE?!
I THOUGHT WE'D RESEALED YOU INSIDE OF JUNJI...!!

MWA HA HA... YOU TRULY BELIEVE THAT A BEING WHO OUTWITTED EVEN THE ANGELS...
WRIGGLE
WRIGGLE
WRIGGLE
WRIGGLE
WRIGGLE
COULD POSSIBLY BE *SEALED* BY THE LIKES OF YOU?

HOWEVER, IF I'D STAYED IN THAT BODY...
IT WOULD'VE ONLY BEEN A MATTER OF TIME BEFORE I WAS EVENTUALLY RESEALED...
FLAP
I REQUIRED A BODY THAT WOULD ALLOW ME FREE USE OF MY MAGIC POWER.

HENCE, I OPTED TO COMMANDEER A BODY ALREADY FULL OF MAGIC POWER-- *YOURS!*
SMIRK

I AM ZIHG ZAHGGER, KING OF DEVILS!!
MASTER OF ALL THE WOMEN IN THE UNIVERSE!!
にょーーん
NYOING
......
NYOING

TAKE THAT!
STOMP
GYAH ?!!

WHOA! IS THIS REALLY HIM?!
WH- WHAT THE HELL DO YOU THINK YOU'RE DOING?!

SQUISH
YOU LITTLE PER-VERT !!
HEY!
GRIND
GET OUT OF MY BODY!! NOW!!
POUND
WAIT!
STOP!

THAT'S IT!! I'VE HAD ENOUGH OF THIS!!
SLITHER
!!
YOU ALREADY BELONG ENTIRELY TO ME!!

YOUR LEGS!
YOUR ARMS!
SLITHER
SLITHER
SLITHER
SLITHER
YOUR FACE!
YOUR HAIR...
AND...

YOUR MELONS !!
SQUEEZE
MY ONE REGRET IS THAT THEY'RE A LITTLE ON THE SMALL SIDE...
GROPE GROPE GROPE GROPE
Somewhere between A and B, huh?
STOOO-OOOP !!
NOW, IF ONLY THEY WERE AS LARGE AS THAT BUSTY ANGEL'S.
SHUT UP, YOU WEIRD LITTLE SLUG !!
THAT'S AS FAR AS YOU GO, DEVIL KING!!
KLOK

I WON'T ALLOW YOU TO DESPOIL ONEESAMA'S BODY ANY FURTHER!
JUST TRY IT AND YOU'LL BE ANSWER-ING TO *ME*!!
DA-DAAN
SERA-SAN...!
OH? "ONEE-SAMA," YOU SAY...?

YOU'RE RATHER CONCERNED FOR THIS GIRL, AREN'T YOU?
CLACK
CLACK
IF YOU DON'T WANT ME TO HAVE THIS BODY...

DOES THAT MEAN I CAN HAVE *YOURS*...?
BA-DUMP
HUH ...?

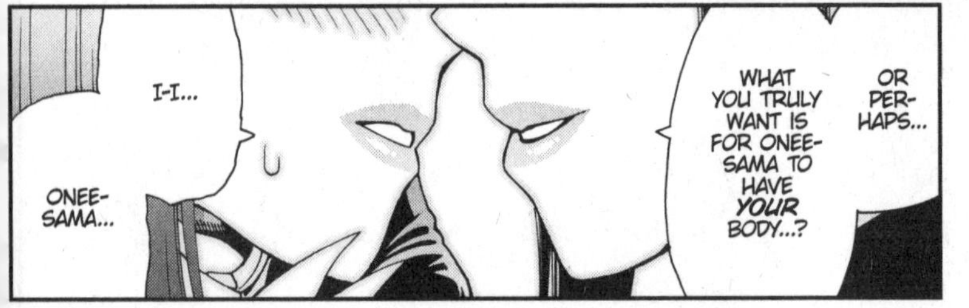
OR PER-HAPS...
WHAT YOU TRULY WANT IS FOR ONEE-SAMA TO HAVE ***YOUR*** BODY...?
I-I...
ONEE-SAMA...

THOUGH, I MUST SAY I MARVEL AT YOUR, *AH*, ANGELIC BOUNTY.
HAH!
AND THIS INTOXI-CATING TEXTURE! *MAGNI-FIQUE!!*
TWITCH
TWITCH
AH!
TWITCH
GROPE
GROPE
AH

AHHHHHHHHH~!
HMPH... ALL TOO SIMPLE.
AH, I SEEM TO RECALL THAT SHE DIDN'T CARE MUCH FOR HER ATTIRE...
SLUMP
I SUPPOSE I SHOULD DIVEST HER OF IT, THEN!
CUT THAT OUT! DON'T DO ANYTHING ELSE WEIRD TO SERA-SAN!!

CRAP... SERA-SAN'S IN DANGER...
BUT HOW CAN I HELP WHEN I CAN'T CONTROL MY OWN BODY...?
DAMN...

HOLD IT RIGHT THERE!!

WHA ...?!

AREN'T YOU GONNA ATTACK ME?!
I CAN TAKE ANYTHING YOU WANNA DISH OUT!!
TROMP
TROMP
CLACK
ZIIIP
TROMP
TROMP
TROMP
TROMP
FIGURES... THAT FRIGGIN IDIOT!!
KWAA
I'D COMPLETELY FORGOTTEN YOU WERE STILL HERE, FORMER VESSEL!!
I HAVE NO NEED FOR MEN!!
SHWMP
AGH!
?!
DWAH?!
BZZT
GWOOSH
TRIP
WHA?!

おおおうえええ!!
BLOOOOOOOOOOORF

KOFF!
BLEH!
UGH...
GAAH!

!!
I'M BACK TO NOR-MAL...?!
H-HOW COULD I BE SO CARELESS?! I *KNEW* I WASN'T COMPLETELY BONDED TO HER BODY YET!
BUT TO BE FORCED OUT BY SOME-THING SO PATHETIC...

I-I HAVE TO HURRY AND GET BACK INTO A BODY...!!
SLITHER
YOINK
?!!

GLARE
GOOOO-TCHAAA!!
WHA?!

HOW DARE YOU PLAY WITH MAKO-CHAN'S BODY SO CASUALLY?!
IT WAS DIRTY OF YOU TO CONTROL HER BODY LIKE THAT!
FEEL THE PAIN OF JUNJI'S ULTIMATE ATTACK!!
YANK!!

(ONE OF) SAGA PREFECTURE TRADITIONA ARTS: SUSURI-MOCHI*!!
DRAG
DRAG
DRAG
DRAG
DRAG
WHAAA?!!
SCREEEEEEEEE

Y-YOU'RE EATING THE DEVIL KING...?!
WHAT ARE YOU DOING?!
MY DAD'S ORIGINALLY FROM SAGA PREFECTURE!!
I KNEW WINNING THAT SUSURI-MOCHI TOURNAMENT WOULD COME IN HANDY!!
GAG!
DRAG
BLEH!
DRAG
DRAG
UH, THAT'S NOT WHAT I MEANT!
WH-WHY, YOU...!!

*Susurimochi: "Slurping mochi," the Saga Prefecture tradition of swallowing long strands of mochi whole instead of chewing it.

YOU HAVE NO IDEA WHAT YOU'RE DOING, HAVE YOU?!
DO YOU UNDER-STAND WHAT INGESTING THE SOUL OF THE KING OF DEVILS WILL *MEAN*?!
BLEH!
THIS TASTE'S NASTY...
NOW THAT I'VE AWOKEN, YOU WON'T BE ABLE TO REPRESS MY OVER-WHELMING MAGIC POWER!!

FROM THIS MOMENT ON, COUNTLESS ANGELS, DEMONS, AND MAGIC-USERS...
WHO'VE CAUGHT WIND OF MY MAGIC POWER...
WILL ATTACK YOU DAY AND NIGHT TO TRY AND CAPTURE MY SOUL!!

WHAT ?!

AN AVERAGE HUMAN SUCH AS YOURSELF WILL NEVER SURVIVE THE ON-SLAUGHT !!
SO, DO YOU *STILL* INTEND TO DEVOUR ME?!

LIKE I GIVE A CRAP ABOUT THAT!!
CHOMP
GYAAA?!!
TWIRL
WIRL
WIRL
WIRL
WIRL
WIRL
DUDE, YOU'RE AN UTTER NOOB WHO ONLY SHOWED UP IN THE LAST CHAP-TER...
LEAVING WHAT YOU DID TO ME ASIDE, HOW DARE YOU TRY TO MAKE MAKO-CHAN YOUR PLAY-THING?!
MAKO-CHAN BELONGS TO ME!!
GACK ...!
SHEESH! WHAT IS WRONG WITH YOU?!
HOW CAN YOU JOKE ABOUT THAT AT A TIME LIKE THIS?!
THIS IS NO TIME TO BE PLAYING AROUND, YA KNOW?!
D-DON'T TELL ME THAT YOU'RE GOING TO...!!

YOU'RE GOING TO SACRIFICE YOUR BODY TO CONTAIN ME...
ALL FOR THE SAKE OF THIS GIRL?!

WHA ...?!

GRIN
HMPH !!
WAH !
YOINK
?!!
W-WAIT !!

I NEVER ASKED YOU TO DO THAT!!
IF ANYTHING EVER HAPPENED TO YOU...
I--

I'LL PROTECT YOU...
MAKO-CHAN!!
KWAA

CHOMP
GYAAAAAAA!!!
AHHH-HHH...
AHH...
AH...
HUH...? BRO?!
IS THIS... MY ROOM...?!
AHA HA HA! SO, YOU'RE AWAKE, JUNJI...

I'M SO RELIEVED. I WAS WORRIED SICK SINCE YOU'D BEEN ASLEEP FOR THREE WHOLE DAYS.
THREE DAYS ?!
NO WONDER I FEEL SO DIZZY.
I WAS STARTING TO WONDER WHETHER SOMETHING EVIL HAD POSSESSED YOU!
TH-THAT'S EXACTLY WHAT HAPPEN-ED!!

THE KING OF DEVILS CAME INTO MY BODY...
Aw, no more tentacles.
THINGS GOT PRETTY CRAZY, AND I HAD TO PULL OUT MY LAST RESORT...
?
BUT IT SEEMS LIKE I'M ALL RIGHT.
RIGHT, MAKO-CHA--

HUH...?
WHAT THE --?
WHERE'S MAKO-CHAN?
SHOULDN'T SHE BE HERE, NURSING ME BACK TO HEALTH?

OH, IF YOU'RE LOOKING FOR TOUDOU-SAN...
SHE LEFT RIGHT AFTER DROPPING YOU OFF HERE THREE DAYS AGO.
SHE HASN'T BEEN BACK SINCE.
WHA ...?!
YOU MUST BE STARVING, HUH, JUNJI?
I'LL GO MAKE YOU SOME RICE POR-RIDGE.
CREAK

N-NOW, WAIT JUST A SEC! WHAT DO YOU MEAN, "HASN'T BEEN BACK"...?!
RUSTLE
AH! YOU SHOULDN'T GET UP SO QUICKLY...!
WOBBLE
"Hasn't" ...?

YOU WERE ASLEEP FOR THREE DAYS. YOU SHOULDN'T PUSH YOURSELF!
KER-CRAASH

ALL RIGHT. YOU JUST STAY PUT, JUNJI.
......

SHE LEFT...?
MAKO-CHAN'S GONE ...?!

SKRCH
SKRCH

HA
AHA
I-I GUESS THAT MAKES PERFECT SENSE!
MAKO-CHAN ONLY CAME HERE TO TAKE HER FINAL EXAM, AFTER ALL!
HA
HA
HA
SHE'S NOT GONNA BE WORRYING ABOUT FINALS WHEN THE KING OF DEVILS IS ON THE LOOSE, AM I RIGHT?!
THERE'S NO WAY SHE CAN MAKE ME A GOOD PERSON IF I'VE GOT THE KING OF DEVILS INSIDE ME, HUH?
OF COURSE NOT! IT ONLY MAKES SENSE!!

WELL! NOW THAT MAKO-CHAN'S GONE, I CAN WATCH ALL THE PORN I WANT!
I'VE GOT A BUNCH OF NEW VIDEOS THAT I COULDN'T WATCH BECAUSE I HAD TO HIDE 'EM!
THE MOTHER-LODE!
WAH HA HA HA...
HA HA...
HA...

FWOO
SNIFF

WHY SO SERIOUS?

MA...
MAKO... CHAN...?
GOOD GRIEF. I TAKE MY EYES OFF OF YOU FOR ONE MOMENT AND YOU'RE BACK TO WATCHING PORN.
GIMME A BREAK... I THOUGHT YOU'D GONE BACK TO THE MAGIC REALM.

I JUST WENT BACK TO DISCUSS THE SITUATION WITH MY PRINCIPAL!
IT'S UNPRECEDENTED FOR THE TARGET OF A SOUL PACT TO BE HOSTING THE SOUL OF THE KING OF DEVILS, AFTER ALL.
It took three whole days just to fill out the paper-work.
SO, I GOT A SPECIAL EXCEPTION TO CHANGE MY FINAL EXAM.

YOU CHANGED...
YOUR FINAL?

STARTING NOW, MY NEW FINAL EXAM...
IS TO PREVENT THE REAWAKENING OF THE KING OF DEVILS...
AND TO GATHER INFORMATION ON HOW TO SEAL HIM AWAY FOR GOOD!!

M...

MAKO-CHAN...!!
STARTLE
SNIFFLE

WH-WHAT'S WITH THAT WEIRD LOOK ON YOUR FACE?!
SNIFF
IT'S... IT'S JUST...

SOB
I WAS AFRAID... I'D NEVER SEE YOU AGAIN...!
I...
SOB
I...
......

YOU SERIOUSLY THINK I'D JUST LEAVE...
WITHOUT SAYING A SINGLE WORD OF THANKS?

UUGH ...!
SNIFFLE

MAKO-CHA--!!
TURN

ONEE-SAMA! WATCH OUT!!
KA-WHAM
STAY BACK, YOU BEAST!!
KONK
?!
ONEESAMA! MY NEW FINAL EXAM IS TO WATCH OVER THE KING OF DEVILS!
CRUMBLE
SO, FROM HERE ON OUT I SHALL PROTECT YOU!!
CRUMBLE
CRUMBLE
JUNJI-SAN, I WON'T ALLOW YOU TO LAY SO MUCH AS A FINGER ON ONEE-SAMA!!
OH?! DOES THAT MEAN I CAN LAY MY FINGERS ON *YOU* INSTEAD...?
NOOOO! HELP, ONEE-SAMA!
SIGH... HOW DID I GET INTO THIS MESS...?
MA MAMA
Until we meet again!

MA MAMA Bonus Manga: The Busty Café of Mira-chan, the Eternal Runner-Up

WHAT?!
THE CLASS PREZ REVIVED A MAID CAFÉ ON THE VERGE OF BANK-RUPTCY...

AND EVEN STARTED A NEW TREND?!

NOT TOO SHABBY, CLASS PREZ!!

BUT THERE'S NO WAY SHE CAN PULL THAT OFF AND I CAN'T!!
I'LL START MY OWN TREND-- BUSTY MAID CAFES!!
JIGGLE
Whoa! Check out those jugs!!
The manager got overconfident and opened a second maid café that's failing.

STANDING ROOM ONLY! I WOULDN'T EXPECT ANY LESS FROM MYSELF!!
PARDON ME, TAKA-SHIRO-SAN.
CLAMOR
CLAMOR

I'VE GOT SOME NEW PRO-SPECTIVE EMPLOY-EES...
But they're, uh...
THEY'VE ALL GOT BIG TITS, RIGHT?!
TROMP
SHOW 'EM IN!

SUMO WRESTLERS
GREET-INGS! OUR BIG TITS ARE AT YOUR SERVICE, MA'AM!!
We're looking for part-time work.

Afterwards, chankonabe* cafés some-how became a new trend.
Hostess, one order of seasonal chanko-nabe!!

HOW DID IT END UP LIKE THIS?!

*Chankonabe is a Japanese stew or hot-pot dish eaten by sumo wrestlers as part of a weight-gain diet.

Breast Review In their P.E. Swimsuits
By OKAYADO
Readers, I love breasts!
Because of this, I made a special corner where I'm going to focus on the breasts of the girls in MaMaMa. I hope you read it to the very end.
By the way, I think I did this because I knew I wouldn't get a chance to have them in their P.E. swimsuits in the actual story.
Mako-chan
B 75, B cup
She's right on the line of veering into 'A cup' territory if she loses even a little bit of weight. Originally, I'd planned on her being secretly well-endowed, but sadly, I had to make her flat-chested.
Huh? B cups aren't flat-chested? La la la...I can't hear you!
3-A TOUDOU
Shun-chan
B 86, E cup
Big boobs with utterly no protection.
Plus, she tends to never wear a bra.
She's not allowed to get wet.
She's a lazy girl and may not even wear underwear.
The author has a habit of making breasts larger and larger with each panel, but does not apologize for this in the least.
KA-POW
You're an 'A cup' today, Mako-chan.
Junji gives Mako-chan's breasts a check-up every morning.

Karin-chan

B 69, AAA cup

Essentially has no breasts.

Mira-chan wearts swimsuits that are too small to make her breasts seem even bigger.

Sera-chan's breasts can't be contained by her shirt, no matter what she does.

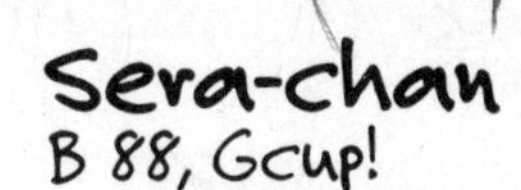

Sera-chan

B 88, Gcup!

Secretly well-endowed loli.
Normally tries to hide how big her breasts are.
Uses a magic bra to make it seem like she's flat-chested.
Who the hell made something so awful?!
What a waste....
I'm sure they show the nipple... at least they should...

Mira-chan

B 95, H cup!

BOOBS!
This is why I wanted her to have more screen time, but I just couldn't fit her in, so she didn't have much of a role. Pretty much from the moment she made her debut, I knew she would be a "rival" (lol). I feel bad for her for a lot of reasons.

MA MAMA

Magical Director Mako-chan's Magical Guidance